kevin's

CHRONICLES

Ron Leath

WARNING: This writing contains some explicit language and small scenes of violence.

DEDICATION

Dedicated to God, my family, and to all those who believed in me.

Ron Leath

Table of Contents

CHAPTER ONE 8

CHAPTER TWO 21

CHAPTER THREE 32

CHAPTER FOUR 44

CHAPTER FIVE 53

CHAPTER SIX......................................60

CHAPTER SEVEN 74

CHAPTER EIGHT 79

CHAPTER NINE..................................84

CHAPTER TEN 94

CHAPTER ELEVEN 102

CHAPTER TWELVE...........................107

CHAPTER THIRTEEN 114

CHAPTER FOURTEEN 125

CHAPTER FIFTEEN...........................131

CHAPTER SIXTEEN 138

CHAPTER SEVENTEEN.....................151

CHAPTER EIGHTEEN 157

CHAPTER NINETEEN 160

CHAPTER TWENTY 164

CHAPTER TWENTY-ONE 173

CHAPTER TWENTY-TWO 185

CHAPTER TWENTY-THREE 188

CHAPTER TWENTY-FOUR 195

About the Author 199

ACKNOWLEDGMENTS

First and foremost, I would like to thank God for blessing me with the talent to write this book. With God, all things are possible. Next, I would like to thank my wife Ebone for being by my side. All the late nights that she spent listening to my ideas and giving me advice has paid off. I would also like to thank my wonderful children: Jahiara and Tahraun for always making me smile and believing that their dad is the greatest dad ever. Special thanks to Jessica Holden and Jessica Barrett for taking the time to read over my work and give great advice. Thanks to my editor, Shatika Turner. Also, my co-workers, Mariel Dorsey and Twaskie Sanders who told me to believe in myself and keep pushing. Very special thanks to Edgar Butler Jr. and Conrad Givers for listening to the story from the beginning. Also, thanks to all who purchase this book. God Bless!

CHAPTER ONE

A Deadly Exchange

Kevin parked directly in front of the old building. His eyes stared into an empty and quiet parking lot. Although the area was calm, his heart wouldn't settle. Each second made him feel like danger was getting closer and closer.

Keep cool, he told himself. Chris was sitting on the other side of him; calm and laid back. He'd been in this situation many times before.

"Man, you're sure we pulled up to the right spot?" Kevin asked.

Chris pulled out his phone and checked the address. "Yep, this it."

It was unusual that Antonio wasn't there yet. Antonio was always on time. And for the slight chance that he wasn't, he would've called by now.

The meet up location was in front of an abandoned

building off of Alameda Street, near downtown Los Angeles. Antonio was the kingpin and they were there to drop off the money to him. This was Kevin's first ride, but Chris had been working with Antonio for years. He asked Kevin to ride along to get acquainted with the operations.

Antonio taught Chris to have a, *trust no one,* state of mind. The longer they waited, the more Chris began to feel that something wasn't right. Either Antonio was already there and testing them, or it wasn't Antonio who called for the meeting.

Kevin had never met Antonio. All he knew was that Chris spoke highly of him. The closest that Kevin has been to a kingpin was watching old Gangsta movies like Scarface and such.

Kevin spotted an alley in front of them. It separated the abandoned building from an office building. "I think we should drive around back," he said to Chris.

Chris nodded. "Yeah, we do need to go back there, but I rather walk through that alley. It'll be easier for me to sneak up on them. But, I'ma give Antonio a few more minutes before I make a move."

Minutes later, a red SUV drove past them and stopped a few feet in front of them at the intersection. Kevin stuck his head out of the window. "You think that's them?"

Chris squinted his eyes as he looked at the vehicle. "That look like my cousin's whip. Da hell he doing ova here?" Chris then opened the car door. As soon as he did, the vehicle sped off and turned the corner towards the direction of the office building. Even though it looked like Henry's car, he wasn't convinced that it was him. He and Henry lived together and were close. There was no way Henry would be in the area and not stop if he saw him.

Just to make sure, he called Henry's phone. It rang and then went to voicemail. "Man, that nigga probably in the house eating Froot Loops and playin' Madden," he joked. "His young ass ain't gonna be in this neighborhood. I told you he ain't built for this shit."

Kevin wasn't so sure. Even if it wasn't Henry, it was still someone. *Why would they stop and then drive off?* he thought. His chest was pounding. He tried to remain calm but could feel his body shaking nervously. "I think we should just leave, bruh," he said to Chris. He tried to say it as manly as possible but he was sure that it didn't come out that way.

"Relax, cuz," Chris replied. "If we leave without giving him the money then shit could get crazy. He obviously wants this money tonight. Otherwise, he wouldn't have hit me up out the blue and told me to meet him."

"So, was it Antonio who hit you up?" Kevin was trying to play detective and piece everything together.

Chris found humor in Kevin's behavior. He felt confident that everything was going to be okay. "Nawl, it was one of his men, but he always doing shit like that. I know it was from him because nobody else got this number, and nobody else knows about the money. Quit trippin' nigga. You scared or something?"

"Nah, man," he lied. "I'm good." He looked to the left to hide his facial expression.

Chris cut on the radio back on. He had Pac's *All Eyes on Me,* in the CD Player. He lit up a blunt and rolled the window down. Since Kevin didn't smoke, he hoped that some west coast, gangsta music could get Kevin to chill.

When he finished smoking, he looked at his watch. Too much time had passed by so he decided that it was time to walk to the back. He got out of the car and opened the trunk. He then pulled out one of the duffel bags of money and walked to the driver's side and left one of the bags with Kevin.

"Look man, I'ma take this one bag to the back. If shit is cool, I'ma text you and you walk through that alley with the other one. Don't come unless I text you, a'ight?"

"Yeah, but are you sure you don't want me to drive, bruh?"

"Nah, Kev. If something crazy going on, or somebody back there who not supposed to be, I want to be able to sneak up on they ass. If we drive back there, then they'll hear us. I got my strap, so we good."

Before he left, he handed Kevin a gun. He knew that Kevin never used one but maybe it would make him feel safer.

"If I ain't back in ten minutes, lock the car and come look for me. Leave the bag unless I tell you to bring it," he ordered.

He nodded in agreement. After Chris walked away, Kevin held the gun in his hand and let out a deep sigh. It didn't make him feel any safer. He just hoped that it would all be over soon.

He kept his eyes on Chris until he disappeared through the alley. It was now 12:14 a.m. Just as he was about to cut the radio volume back up, his phone rang. It was his girl, Nia. Once he answered, she immediately started yelling at him. She had been through a lot that day and was wondering where he was. He left the house when she fell asleep and she woke up looking for him.

He for sure didn't want to tell her where he was, though. As far as she knew, he was out the game for good. He let out a sigh and quickly made up a lie. He was hoping that she would be okay with that and get off the phone. However, she didn't believe him. She was still emotional about the bad news that she had found out earlier. All she wanted was for him to come home. She begged him to come back as quickly as he could.

He was eager to get off the phone. "Bae, I promise I'll be home within thirty minutes. Just lay back down," he said to her.

Suddenly, a white Cadillac approached from behind. Kevin was looking down at his phone since he had it on speaker mode. A woman was driving the car and another female was in the passenger's seat. A guy sat in the back, holding a gun.

Kevin's eyes were still looking down as they slowly drove past him. The Cadillac turned the same way that the red SUV did earlier.

Kevin looked up just in time to catch the tail end of the car. He was positive that it was the same car that was following him earlier near Chris's house.

He looked at his watch and it was 12:27. More than ten minutes had passed since Chris left. He quickly got out of the car while still on the phone with Nia.

She could hear the panic in his voice. "Kevin, why do you sound worried, and what's all that noise in the background?" She asked.

"Nothing, bae, I gotta go. I'll be home soon." He hung up and put the phone in his pocket.

He left the bag of money in the car and grabbed the gun. He hesitantly walked towards the alley. It was dark. The only light was coming from the third floor of the office building. As he was about halfway through his journey, he heard some people talking so he stopped to listen. It sounded like a few different voices, but it was too faint to really hear whose voice it was. All the voices were coming from the back side of the building.

Once the voices ceased, he started walking again, but stopped once more when he heard a growing sound and saw what he thought was a shadow of a person.

"Chris, that's you?" he whispered.

No one answered. When he looked up again, the shadow was gone and the area was quiet again. His chest rose and fell with rapid breaths. His first thought was that someone was going to roll up on him. He still had the gun in his hand so he took a few more steps. He was almost to the end of the alley and then his phone vibrated.

"Shit!" The sudden movement had him shook. He looked at his phone and it was a text message from Chris. He calmed him down as he read the message. *I'm back here with Antonio. Bring the other bag.*

He quickly turned around and walked to the car to get the other bag. When he got to the trunk, he pulled the bag out and put the straps over his shoulders. Within a quick second, he felt a presence behind him. He was just about to turn around to see who it was, but then he felt a metal object on the back of his head.

"Yeah nigga, you know what time it is," a deep voice said. "Run that shit."

Kevin lifted his left hand up and then slid the bag off his right shoulder. He was shaking. He knew he could be shot at any minute.

The person holding the gun snatched it from him. "Too easy," he laughed as he kneeled down to unzip the bag.

Kevin turned around slightly and saw that the stranger had a mask on. "Fuck," he whispered. His gun was in his coat pocket.

He tried to ease his hand down, but the man saw him. He got up and pressed the gun to the back of Kevin's head again. "Move again and I'ma bust yo' ass," he warned. His voice had enough base in it for Kevin to know that he was serious. At that point, Kevin recognized the voice but couldn't match a face with it.

The gunman kneeled again and started counting the money. Kevin stayed still with his hands up. Once he finished counting, he made a phone call. "It's all there, Slim. Bout to take care of this fool and head to the back."

Henry! Kevin said to himself. That's whose voice it was. *Chris's cousin.* He heard Slim's name also. He didn't know what to think. All he knew was he needed to confront him. He slowly turned around and faced him. Henry locked eyes with him and zipped the bag and stood up. Kevin had a look of anger on his face. Henry now knew that his identity had been revealed. He took off his mask. He still had the gun pointed at Kevin.

"Business is business, cuz. You and Chris tried to stop my hustle. Now I gotta do you like I did him."

Kevin reacted quickly. He charged towards Henry. A gunshot went off, but no one got hit. They wrestled and the gun slid on the ground a few feet away. Henry overpowered Kevin and slammed him to the ground. Henry ran for the gun, but just as he picked it up, Kevin reached into his pocket and pulled out his. Before Henry could fire a shot, Kevin closed his eyes and squeezed the trigger. He heard a painful sound coming from Henry. He opened his eyes just as Henry was falling to the ground. He was covered in blood.

Kevin panicked. He kneeled next to him and put his hand over his chest to try to stop the bleeding. "Henry, da hell is going on man and what happened to Chris?" he cried out to him. "What you mean by *do you like I did him?*"

Henry didn't respond. He was trying to but struggled to breathe. He closed his eyes and the gasping for air stopped. Henry appeared to be dead.

Kevin was frozen in disbelief. "Fuck!" he shouted, realizing he had just taken a life. He snapped out of it when he heard someone approaching from the other side of the building. It was Slim. He ran behind the car to avoid getting spotted. When Slim came to the area where Henry's body was lying, he stopped and drew his gun. He turned his head in all directions, trying to see if anyone else was around. Once he felt that the coast was clear, he reached over Henry's motionless body and picked up the bag. He didn't check to see if Henry was breathing. Once he put the bag over his shoulders, he jogged back around the building.

Kevin sprinted towards the alley in hopes of getting back there before Slim did. When he got there, he saw

Henry's car and the white Cadillac from earlier. There was no sign of Chris. He spotted a woman sitting in the driver's seat of the white car. She was looking down, so she didn't see Kevin approaching at first. He slowly walked towards the car with his pistol in his hand. After a few steps, he felt a presence behind him again.

"P-Put the gun down," someone stuttered. It was the voice of a woman. He turned around and sat the gun down slowly. It frightened him even more knowing that she was so nervous. He thought that if he made one slight move, she would just shoot. *A scared person is a dangerous person.*

"I-ain' trying to hurt anyone," he pleaded. "I'm just trying to find out what happened to my homeboy so we can get outta here. If it's about the money, y'all can have it all."

She was still shaking while pointing the gun at him. He kept his hands lifted. Slim emerged from the side of the building. He saw Kandy pointing the gun at Kevin and he yelled for her to shoot him. As she turned and looked at Slim, Kevin quickly stepped to her and grabbed the gun away from her. She struggled with him and the gun went off. Her fingers slid off the gun and she fell to the ground. She was shot and blood was pouring from her shirt.

Slim saw the whole thing from a distance and he tried to retaliate. He starting shooting at Kevin. There was a small electric box near one of the parking spaces so Kevin ran behind it and started shooting back.

Slim was carrying the bag of money that he got from Henry. He fired two more shots then ran out of bullets. Kevin was still shooting. Slim ran towards the white Cadillac but dropped the bag as he tried to hurry. He had no time to get it. He already had one of the bags near the car, so he picked it up and jumped in the car and they drove off.

Kevin came from behind the box and walked up to the girl who was just shot. He couldn't believe that Slim would leave her there to die. She was gasping for air. She tried to speak but every word came out as a struggling stutter. She pointed towards the dumpster to the right of them. Kevin looked over there but didn't see anything or anyone. "What's over there?" he asked her.

She was able to muster the strength to say, "Sorry," before she closed her eyes and took her last breath.

His emotions were all over the place. He was scared, angry and anxious all at the same time. Although he was defending himself, two people were shot dead by his hands.

To see what she was pointing at, he looked closely towards the dumpster again. This time, he saw someone lying on the ground. His first thought was that it was Chris. He ran over there and confirmed it. Chris's eyes were closed, and his shirt was covered in blood from what appeared to be stab wounds.

"No!" Kevin shouted. Kevin shook him in hopes that he would wake up, but it was too late. What was supposed to be a simple deal turned out to be a tragic night. Chris taught him everything he knew about the streets.

Sirens were approaching so he got one last look at Chris and shook his head as he ran off. He saw the bag of money that Slim dropped so he picked it up and ran through the alley with it. He jumped in his car and drove off but when he passed Henry, he didn't realize that he was still breathing.

CHAPTER TWO

Time For a Change

Three months earlier...

Kevin was depressed. Bills were piling up and he didn't have a steady income to support Nia. She was working full-time, but it wasn't enough. They only had one car and were behind on the payments. The only hope was that he was a few months from finishing his Music Production degree. His dreams of landing a job as a music producer were appearing to be close.

One day, he was sitting in the living room chilling and watching TV and looked out the window and saw the mailman outside. He was expecting a letter from one of the record companies that he'd sent samples of his beats to. After the mailman finished, he walked outside to grab the mail. When he came back inside, he sifted through it and his eyes lit up in excitement when he saw a letter from one of the local record companies. He couldn't wait to open it.

"Nia come in here!" he shouted. "I got a letter from one of these record companies! I'ma bout to open it."

He was too excited. Nia was in the bathroom getting dressed for work. "Go ahead and open it sweetie," she yelled back to him. "I'll be out there in a minute."

He opened it and his eyes skipped over the introduction part. He went straight to the next paragraph that gave their review on his material. After reading the first line, he ripped the paper up and threw it on the floor. It stated that they were not interested.

Nia heard the commotion and walked into the living room. She saw his face and knew he had received some bad news. She walked over to the couch and sat on his lap. She ran her fingers through his dreads. She hated to see him down. "Baby, you are good at what you do and your hard work will pay off one day. You're already selling your beats in the streets. Keep doing what you do and these companies will take notice."

"Yeah, but I ain't making shit off the streets. I'm trying to get paid and I can't sell a beat for more than fifty right now. I wanna least make a couple hunid off each one."

She was still upbeat. "Kevin, we will be ok, God will make a way. My overtime is about to kick back in."

"Bae, you already doing enough. I need to do more. I gotta find a part time job or something."

"Kevin, I got this," she replied. "All I want you to do is finish school and worry about work after you graduate. Until then, let me take care of things."

He let out a sigh of frustration. It made him feel less than a man since she was the only one bringing in a steady income. What made it worse was the fact that they were two months behind on rent. "I hear ya, bae. But I gotta make some moves. This rent ain't gon' pay itself."

"Kevin, if you that concerned about rent, then why don't we live with my auntie for a while? She suggested it last time we were over there. She's closer to your school and closer to my job anyway. We won't have to pay her anything."

He shook his head and let out a smirk. "Man, what I look like having two women take care of me. That's lame as hell."

"Kevin, sometimes you have to take a step back before you can move forward. Imagine shooting a bow without pulling it back, it won't go nowhere, but if you pull it back like you supposed to, then it will shoot out far. That's what we need to do."

He smiled at her. "Girl, you know how to say the right thangs. That's why I love you so much. I can't promise anything, but if all else fails, I will consider it. Let me try to make some moves first."

She rested her head on his chest. "Well, just don't let nothing get in the way of your passion."

She was so in love with him. He was muscular, chocolate-skinned, and tall, but what she loved the most was the fact that he was smart and well-rounded. She didn't want anyone else but him.

She stretched her body out and relaxed on him. She didn't get a chance to get fully dressed so she only had on a T-shirt and a pair of panties. Her warm body made him aroused. He rubbed her legs in admiration. He felt blessed to have such a dedicated, independent and beautiful woman. Nia had a high-yellow skin complexion and it was soft and smooth. Her waist was small, but she had wide hips, with a matching butt and big breasts. The main physical feature that he loved about her was her plumped lips that she kept glossy and smooth.

He was hoping to get some, so he lifted her shirt and started kissing her body. She started moaning and began to rub her hand all over his back. As soon as he stood up to take off his shirt, there was a loud knock at the front door. Nia put her hand over her breasts. "Who's at the door, Kevin?"

Kevin looked at the wall clock. He had class today so he figured that it was Jessica there to pick him up. He took a look through the peephole and confirmed that it was her. Nia walked to the room to put on some clothes and Kevin opened the door.

Jessica and Kevin met when they were paired on assignments at school. They became best friends. Since Kevin and Nia only had one car, she would often come pick him up and drop him off. Nia was cool with her as well.

Jessica had her usual smile on her face when she walked in. She had a pecan-brown complexion and a great body, but it was always hidden under loose jeans and T-shirts. She was very attractive but never liked to draw attention to herself. She wasn't dating anyone, she only wanted to focus on school.

She noticed that Kevin had on house-clothes. "Boy, did you forget about school? You know we can't be late; we got a rap group coming in to record today."

"My bad. Me and Nia got caught up in a lil convo."

She chuckled. "Umm hmm. Convo with your shirt off? Yeah, ok."

He went to the back to change clothes. Nia came into the living room a few minutes later and talked to Jessica. She complimented Jessica on her makeup and nails. They engaged in a conversation while waiting on Kevin.

After Kevin got dressed, he walked into the living room, kissed Nia and he and Jessica headed out for class. During the ride, she asked him how things were going and he told her about the money situation. She suggested that he should apply for a position at the grocery store where she worked. It was a part-time gig but at least it was flexible. He agreed and made plans to go there sometime that week. He could sure use the income.

Minutes later, they reached their destination. They were doing an internship at a music studio in Watts, and that's where they would remain until graduation. Jessica was training to become a recording engineer, which focused more on the technical side of recording music and

Kevin was training to become a music producer. They both were talented and worked well together.

When they walked inside, they were greeted by Mark, the senior producer. He had them set up the mics and other equipment for the group. Kevin was hoping that the group needed some beats, so he came up with a pitch to try and sell at least one to them. The group arrived about ten minutes later. There were three of them. Two of the guys went inside the booth and the third one took a seat behind Kevin and Jessica.

He introduced himself as Mike. He was tall, dark-skinned, with dreads and a goatee. He had a nice, cool, laid-back vibe. He and Jessica cut eyes at each other a few times.

The other two were rappers and he was just managing them. He then handed Kevin a CD with some beats on it. The group were going to use them to record their songs on.

Kevin looked at the CD before loading it. "Did you make these beats?"

"Nah, we're using some industry beats for right now. Right now, I'm just trying to show people that these boys can spit. Once I build my own studio, I'm gonna be lookin' for somebody who can make some fire beats."

Kevin chimed in on the opportunity. "Man, I got them fire beats," he cheesed. "I've been making beats since I was like 14." He played a few of them on his laptop for him.

Mike really liked the beats. He was just a street dude looking to make some legit money through rap. He met the two rappers when they were doing a show at a local club. He decided to put a little money behind them and wanted them to record more songs. They had good talent and he was expecting them to blow up pretty soon.

He offered to buy the beats from Kevin. Kevin told him one-fifty apiece. To his surprise, Mike was cool with it. They didn't use the beats for this session because it didn't go with the songs they were recording, but he told him that he would definitely be back. He then pulled out a stack of cash and handed Kevin three, one hundred-dollar bills. Kevin burned him a CD and gave him the beats. After that, it was back to business and the group recorded their songs. Once they finished, Jessica started mixing it and Kevin stepped outside to call Nia.

"Look at God!" she shouted when she heard the news. I told you it'll all work out for us. Just keep pushing."

This made him forget all about the bad news that he got in the mail. He was more focused now. "Yeah, you're right. I'ma just stick with it. Dude said that they're gonna be needing more beats from me in the future, so hopefully the money keeps rolling in."

"It will, boo. And listen, I gotta go. Some customers came in. I'll see you when I get off tonight. Love you."

"Alright, coo'. Love you too."

He went back inside and thanked Mike again for buying the beats. Once the tracks were loaded, Jessica took over the session. There was nothing else for him to do so he grabbed her car keys and sat inside while he waited on her.

As he waited, he heard a car approaching that was playing loud music. It was an old-school, blue Chevy Impala and it stopped at the light across from him. The top was down a big dark-skinned man was driving. He had on a white tee and a huge, shiny gold necklace wrapped around his neck. When the light turned green, the driver made a U-turn and parked in front of some houses across the street from the studio. A woman walked outside with a few dollars in her hand. She walked up to the car and handed him the money. He gave her a small bag in exchange. Once the exchange was done, the driver pulled into the studio's parking lot. He parked into an empty space right next to Kevin. Kevin got an up-close look at his whip. The blue paint was shiny and the rims were clean.

The man looked around as if he was waiting on someone. Kevin paid it no mind and just continued to scroll through his phone and listen to music. About thirty minutes later, Mike and the two rappers came out and walked to the guy's car. They dapped him up and jumped in the ride. Before they pulled off, Mike looked over at Kevin. "Preciate those beats, fam. I'll be in touch."

"Fa sho." They drove off and Jessica came out a few minutes later. She saw a smile on Kevin's face. "What you grinning about?" she asked.

"Man, they're doing big thangs."

She thought he was referring to the music. "Yeah, they do sound nice."

"Nah, I'm talking about whatever else they doing. They just got picked up by some dude in a blue Six-fo and I saw him make a drug sale across the street. All of them had on nice clothes. I need in on their operations."

She sucked her teeth. "You don't need none of that, Kevin. Stay focused with this music. This is how we gonna get paid."

The drive to his place was silent. Jessica had other things on her mind and all Kevin could think about was money. He was tired of struggling and seeing everyone else with nice things.

When Jessica dropped him off, he walked up to his floor. Just as he thought that things couldn't get any worse, he found an eviction letter taped to the door. He snatched it off and punched the door as hard as he could.

Receiving money for the beats was the highlight of his day, but it seemed like every time something went right in his life, it was following by something ten times worse. He needed to come up with two months of rent within the next 10 days. On top of that, the new rent was due in 8 days. Unless a miracle happened, he had no other alternatives.

CHAPTER THREE

A Change of Plans

After getting evicted, Kevin and Nia moved in with her aunt, Shirley. She lived near the intersection of Wilmington Avenue and Santa Ana Boulevard. Nia's overtime didn't work out as planned, so after talking it over with Kevin, they both felt it was the best move for them. Her aunt was the only family that stayed in California. The rest of Nia's family was in Texas and Kevin's family was in Florida.

Shirley was glad to have them stay with her. She lived in a three-bedroom house, so she had plenty of room. Their bedroom was in the front part of the house and they had their own bathroom. The living room was to the right. A long hallway separated the rest of the house.

The kitchen was next down the hall and then the other two bedrooms were behind it.

Nia had to go to work the same day that they moved in, but she checked on Kevin before she left. "Hey, how you doing, hun?" He was stretched out on the sofa. "I'm fine, boo. Just gonna relax and chill for a little bit."

Nia knew Kevin didn't want to be there, but she could tell that he was trying to stay positive. "Kevin, trust me, we will have our own place again in no time. Auntie said that we don't have to give her anything, but I'ma give her something for the lights and stuff. We'll be able to buy our own food."

"Aight cool, bae. Have a good day at work." He wasn't trying to rush her out; he just didn't want to hear that at the moment. The fact that he was staying with someone else made him feel less than a man.

About an hour later, Jessica called him and gave him some good news. She spoke with her manager and said that he could come in for an interview that same day. They had to go to class but the interview was scheduled a few hours before so they had plenty of time.

He hurried to the closet and picked out his best suit. Matter of fact, it was the only one that he could still fit. He got it from K&G a few years back but he still wore it from time to time. Going to a grocery store interview with a suit on was a little rare, but he wanted to dress to impress.

Once he got dressed, he looked in the mirror and quickly gained confidence. He was already confident that he would get the job, but now he was confident that everything would all work out. Nia wouldn't have to work so hard anymore.

Jessica arrived and knocked on the door. She lived only three streets from Nia's aunt. Kevin came out with a huge, Kool-Aid smile.

"Look at you," she complimented. "You look nice."

"Thanks. Just trying to go in there lookin' fresh, feel me?"

Jessica loved his sense of humor. She too was confident that he would get the job. He now had the right attitude.

When they arrived, she walked him to the office to meet Chuck, her manager. After they greeted, she went back to the car to wait on him. Chuck was a heavy-set, balding man and wore glasses. He wasn't as cheerful as Kevin remembered Jessica telling him he was. "Have a seat," he said sternly to Kevin. As he looked over his application, he started shaking his head. "So, I see that you haven't had a job in over a year, and that was in Florida."

"Yes sir," Kevin responded in an upbeat manner. "I moved here last year to go to school and that's been my focus."

Chuck sat the application down. Either he was in a bad mood or just wasn't too impressed with Kevin. He kept looking at Kevin's dreads. It was followed by a brief moment of silence.

Kevin broke the ice. "Is everything good, sir? Do you have any questions about my past jobs? I can definitely come in on time and work as many hours as you need me to."

Chuck tilted his head forward and his glasses slid off of his face slightly. He locked eyes with Kevin. Showing little emotion, he spoke. "I can start you off working around two days a week, and about four to five hours a day."

Kevin scrunched his face. That was eight to ten hours a week. Jessica was working full-time so he thought he would get at least twenty hours. "Sir, I need more hours than that," he pleaded. "Me and my girl trying to save up to get our own place again."

Chuck folded his arms. "Sorry, but that's the best that I can do for right now. Jessica's been with me for a while and she worked her way up to full-time. Just try it out and we'll see how it goes after a couple of months."

Kevin sucked his teeth. "If that's all you got then no thanks, I'm good. I can't live on that kinda money."

Chuck remained stern. "Are you sure about that?"

"I'm positive. It'll be a waste of time to come all the way out here for some chump change." Kevin mumbled something else under his breath before storming out.

Chuck's attitude was the main reason he didn't accept it. He couldn't imagine working for an asshole like him. They would bump heads all the time.

Jessica was waiting in the car for him. She saw the look on his face. "How'd it go?" she asked.

"Man, fuck Chuck." He avoided eye contact with her. He stared out the window as she drove away.

"What do you mean *fuck* him? Did you take the job or what?"

"No, I didn't" he steamed. "That muthafucka talking about ten hours a week. Nah, fuck that."

Jessica had a disgusted facial expression as she turned her head towards him. "Kevin, I told you he always says that to people during their interview. As soon as you get on the floor, he will raise your hours."

"Raise my hours to what? 15? Plus, it's minimum wage. I-ain' bout ta' bust my ass for no lil bit of change. He gotta come better than that. I need to get paid."

"Kevin, where did all this *wanting money* talk come from? You've been tripping lately."

"Look, I'm just trying to get paid. It seems like everybody else doing good except me."

"Kevin, y'all are living with Nia's aunt, so stop worrying about money so much. Once we're done with school, I'm sure you will have all kinds of job offers to become a music producer."

That was too far in the future for him to think about right now. The reality was, he was broke and living off his girlfriend and her aunt. No one understood his struggles. Everyone kept telling him to relax and just focus on music. That was hard to do when he had a girlfriend who came home tired from working all day. Something had to change.

"Drop me off at the crib," he said to her.

"So, you're not going to class?"

"Man, I'ain' in the mood for that shit today. I need to rest for a little while."

Jessica shook her head and sighed. She figured that he would get over it soon. She turned down his street and dropped him off at the corner. He got out and walked to the house without saying bye to her.

When he got there, he decided to just sit on the porch. He didn't want to be cramped up in a room. It would make him more depressed.

He called Nia while she was at work. "Aye bae, what you doing?" he said as she answered. He was still upset but was trying not to reveal his frustration.

Nia was her usual self. Upbeat and cheerful. "Nothing, tired and ready to go. How was the interview?"

"I didn't get it." He didn't bother explaining to her why he didn't, because he knew that she wasn't going to question it anyway.

"Don't worry, boo," she replied "I told you that everything will still work out for us."

"I hope so. I just want you to keep praying for us, Nia. We need it."

She let out a chuckle. "Oh, I am. And hey, let's do something fun tonight. Let's go to City Walk tonight. We haven't been out in a minute."

He glanced around just before he spoke. He really wasn't in the mood to do anything. "I mean, can we afford it? I ain't got no money."

"Uggh, yes, Kevin. Parking is free after nine, I think. We can just walk around and get something to eat. Or we can do whatever. I just want to get out the house."

"Ok, cool. Well, get back to work. Love ya."

"Love you too, Kevin. Bye."

He was still sitting on the porch and he saw two guys walk outside from a house across the street. One of them lit up a blunt and kept looking around as if they were waiting on someone. A few moments later, a car pulled up and parked in front of them. Kevin noticed that it was the same Impala that he saw a couple of weeks ago when he met Mike at the studio.

Three people were inside of the car and they all got out. It was the same driver that he saw last time. He also saw Mike. He hadn't seen or heard from him since the day he sold him the beats.

He walked off the porch and stood by the fence of his yard and spoke to him. "Sup Mike," he yelled.

Mike squinted his eyes but didn't immediately recognize him. "Who is you, nigga? Ion know nobody who stay over there."

By this time, all of them turned and stared at Kevin. One of them lifted their shirt up, revealing a gun. Before anything popped off, Kevin walked to the middle of the street in hopes that Mike would realize who he was. "Aye, this Kev from the studio."

Recognition then dawned on Mike. "Oh, shit Kev!" he declared. "Maaan, come over here and meet the homies."

Kevin walked over to the yard and the first person that Mike introduced him to was a man named Slim; the driver of the Impala. Slim had the look of a real gangster. He stood about six feet, four inches and weighed at least three hundred pounds. He had on a L.A. jersey, some shorts and that same big gold chain that he had on last time. Tattoos covered both of his arms and he had a few around his neck. Kevin was smiling when he shook his hand, but it was all serious-face for Slim.

The next person he introduced him to was Frank. He told Kevin that he and Frank had known each other since the third grade. They were also roommates and lived down the street. Frank was cool and laid-back. He was short and chubby and had a low haircut. He offered to let Kevin hit the blunt, but he told him that he didn't smoke.

One of the guys went back into the house before Kevin had a chance to speak to him. There was one other guy remaining. He was a tall, skinny, brown-skinned dude who had braids. He looked pretty young. Kevin was only twenty-three and he looked younger than him. When Mike introduced them, he told him that the young dude's name was Henry. Henry was quiet and didn't say much. He walked into the house a few minutes later.

"I don't care for that nigga," Mike said to Kevin about Henry. "He's my homeboy's lil cousin but something is up with him. Nigga strange as hell."

They walked away from the others and started talking about music.

"Bruhhh," Mike said while putting his arm on his shoulder. "Me and Frank just got some state-of-the-art equipment. I'm working with the dude who owns the fish market so we can rent out the building behind him. I'ma turn that bitch into a studio."

"Nice," Kevin nodded. "I can't wait till you hear some more of my beats."

"Bet. We're gonna move quick so expect everything to pop off in about two to three weeks. I need them fire beats, cuzzo."

As they continued to talk, Nia's aunt pulled up. She opened her trunk and started getting some of the groceries out but turned her head towards them when she heard them talking. She squinted her eyes and looked over and saw Kevin. She shook her head. "Kevin, I need your help," she yelled.

He jogged over and took the groceries inside for her. Once he was done, he tried to go back outside, but she stopped him before he got out the door. "Kevin, let me talk to you, it will on take a second."

"Okay," he said while turning around and walking into the living room with her. He had a feeling that it was about him being across the street.

Before she could get another word out, she started coughing uncontrollably. It was a barking type of cough and she whistled a sound at the end of each cough, gasping for air. He panicked. "You ok, Miss Shirley?"

After clearing her throat, the coughing slowly ceased. "Yes, baby I'm fine. I gotta get ready to take this medicine soon."

She started talking to him about the guys across the street. "Kevin, I don't know what you were doing out there, but I can tell you that those guys are trouble. You don't need to fool with them. Not too long ago, they had a shootout with some other gang, and the police are over there all the time. The one who drives the blue car with the big tires is the worst one. I see him all up and down the streets selling drugs. Don't get caught up in that mess."

Kevin tried to defend himself. "I'm definitely not involved with him, auntie. The other guys do music so we were trying to connect on that."

"Well, all of them are bad, Kevin. The one who lives there is sneaky too. I had a run-in with him a while back. I told him to keep the noise down. His girlfriend pulled up as we were talking and she stared me down like she was about to jump on me or something. I'm telling you, everybody over there is dangerous."

Kevin took in what she was saying, but he only saw them as an opportunity to make money with music. He didn't care about anything else that they were doing.

CHAPTER FOUR

Money Moves

Nia was in a good place in her life. She had all that she could want. A good man, a job and family who supported her. Living with her aunt turned out to be a good thing for them. She now had money saved up and was going to eventually surprise Kevin by getting them their own place again.

As she sat in the living room, she heard her aunt come out of her room and go in the kitchen. She went in there to talk to her. "Hey, Auntie, what cha' doing?"

Aunt Shirley couldn't hear that well so she turned around when she heard someone talking. She then noticed that it was Nia. "Oh hey, baby. Just bout to fix me a glass of juice. I need to wash these dishes."

"Oh, don't worry about that, Auntie. Kevin said that he will wash them, but since I'm off today, I may end up doing it."

Shirley smiled. "Thank you, baby, I hope Kevin realizes how lucky he is to have a woman like you."

"Oh, he does, Auntie. He tells me all the time."

Shirley was a very caring aunt. She knew Nia had a good head on her shoulders and was good at making the right decisions, but she wanted to know more about Kevin. Him being outside with those guys the other day still didn't sit right with her. She knows that they are in love, but she just wants to make sure that Kevin has his head on straight.

"Sit down, baby," she said to Nia as she poured her juice. "Let's talk."

Nia put the juice in the fridge for her and then sat next to her. "What's up, Auntie?"

Shirley took a sip and clenched her face when the coldness hit her teeth. "Nia, how are you and Kevin really doing? I know y'all been down here for a year now and all, but are things going good?"

"Yes, things are really good. A lot of stress has been taken away from us now that we are living here."

"Umm hmm, I see. Well, that's good. But I have a question, did he tell you that I caught him talking to them guys across the street?"

Nia jerked her neck back. "No. You talking about over there at that house where all those cars be at?"

"Yes. He was over there last week. That was Angie's house. Angie and I were good friends. She died a while back. Her only child, Chris, lives there now with her sister's son. He was in prison when she died. The house was up for sale, but I guess he bought it or something. And ever since he got out, they've been doing all kinds of crazy mess over there."

Nia lifted her eyebrow. "And you say Kevin was over there?"

"Yeah, he was. I told him to stay away from them and he mentioned something about doing music with them. I don't know but just make sure he's not over there all the time."

"Ok, Auntie, I will definitely talk to him."

Kevin was always upfront about who he hung with or talked to, so this was a surprise to Nia. She planned on having a conversation with him about it.

Someone knocked on the door as they talked. Nia got up and hurried to the door.

"Who is it?" she asked.

"This Mike. Kev home?"

Nia opened the door, leaving the security chain on. "Yes, he's here." She raised her head, waiting for him to say what he wanted with him.

"Cool. He sold me some beats a while back. I just wanted to holla at him about some music."

"Hold on." Nia closed the door and walked in the room to get him. He was sitting at his computer desk. She waited until he took his headphones off before saying anything.

"Kevin, someone named Mike is at the door for you."

"Alright, bet." He already knew what time it was. He grabbed his laptop and headed for the door.

She stuck her hand out and stopped him. "That better not be one of them guys my auntie told you to stay away from."

Awe transformed his face. "What you mean?"

"Umm hmm," she said. "Don't play dumb, she told me that you were out there talking to them a couple of weeks ago."

Kevin shook his head. "There you go. Look bae, I don't know what these guys are doing and I really don't care. Only thing I care about is selling these beats. That's gonna mean dollas coming in."

She raised her voice a little. "Kevin, stop worrying about money so much. We're doing good. Don't get caught up in that mess just to get some money."

"I'm not," he snapped back. "I'ma' let him hear a couple more beats and that's about it."

She didn't want him to go but gave in. He kissed her on the cheek and went outside with Mike.

Mike had a huge smile on his face. "Kev, the studio is all set up, cuz. We got a bunch of shit in there."

"Word? Shid', when can I check it out?"

"You can come through now, playa."

Mike only lived a block away, so they walked over there. The rappers, Sean and Quentin were already in the booth. Kevin also saw another guy who he'd never seen before. He was tall, thin, light-skinned and had his hair braided.

Mike introduced them. "Kev, this is my homeboy, my ace, Chris. We've been down for a long ass time. He's the one that live across the street from you; Henry's cousin."

Chris was cool and reserved. He carried himself like Mike did. He complimented Kevin on the beats and said that they will definitely be working with him on a regular basis.

They recorded on one of Kevin's beats that he gave them the first time. He was excited. He knew that the way they flowed, it would match the beat perfectly. If they were able to get it out to people, it would probably become a hit.

As they recorded, Mike started a conversation with Chris. Kevin listened in.

"I'm really 'bout to get rid of this nigga," Chris said to Mike. "I'on give a fuck if I've known him for ten days or ten years. If you ain't delivering the dope on time, then we have a problem."

They were referring to Slim. Slim had been coming up short lately and wasn't selling all the dope that he got from them.

"We can't let that shit ride," Mike added.

Frank came in and slammed the door behind him. He walked over to Chris without speaking to the others. "I need to holla at you outside."

They walked out the back door. The rappers continued to record and Mike started a conversation with Kevin in between sessions. He told him some of the plans that they were trying to come up with in the upcoming months regarding music.

"Man, y'all doing big thangs," Kevin said to him.

Mike grinned. "Hell yeah, this the year of getting paid, cuzzo. If you stick with us, you gonna get paid in no time, bruh. Just make sure you get in good with my nigga, Chris. He can get you paid from other thangs too, you feel me?"

"Fa sho." Kevin didn't know what *other things* that he was referring to but any money coming in would be good. It was about time for a come up so he wanted to stick with them and do whatever that needed to be done.

A little while later, Nia texted him and told him that it was time for her aunt's doctor appointment. Mike was moving some of the volume levels down when Kevin stood up. "You bout to ride, homie?"

"Yeah, man. My girl wants me to ride with her to take her aunt to the doctor. I'ma slide back through either tonight or tomorrow."

Mike gave him dap. "Yeah, come fuck with us anytime, bruh."

As he walked out, he saw Chris standing outside on the phone. Frank had already left. Kevin didn't want to interrupt his conversation, so he threw up a peace sign and walked off. Chris got off the phone and jogged towards him.

"Hol' up, Kev let me holla at cha."

Kevin stopped and waited for him to come over. He could tell by the effort, that he had something important to tell him.

"Aye Kev, so you an intern at the studio up the street, right?"

"Yeah, something like that. Sup?"

Chris rubbed his hands together. "Listen man, Mike told me that he trusts you a lot and shit. I was wondering if you could drop a bag off to a house right across the street from the studio."

Kevin's forehead creased. "What kinda bag?"

"For right now, it's probably best if we don't talk about all the details, but I swear, it ain't nothing to be worried about. It's really no risk."

Before Kevin could answer, Chris walked inside of the studio and came back out with a duffel bag. He also pulled out some money from his pocket and handed Kevin five hundred dollars.

"This yours if you can do that for me, cuz."

Kevin's eyebrows rose. "Damn, just for a bag? So, am I just gonna hand it to someone?"

"Nope. Yeen gotta talk to nobody," Chris explained. "All you gotta do is drop it off and pick up an envelope. Cool?"

It sounded very simple. Kevin looked at the bag then looked at Chris. It only took him a few seconds to come up with an answer. He put the money in his pocket and grabbed the bag.

CHAPTER FIVE

The First Job

Kevin hid the bag behind the sofa to keep it away from Nia and her aunt. When he woke up the next morning, Nia was still asleep and Aunt Shirley was in her room. He had class that day so after he got dressed, he kissed Nia goodbye and grabbed the bag on his way out. He then waited outside for Jessica to pick him up. She texted and said she was running a little late. *Damn.* Kevin was ready to go. He didn't want to risk Nia or her aunt coming outside and seeing the bag.

Ten minutes later, Nia came outside. He slid the bag out of the way with his foot. She stood by the screen door, stretching and yawning. "Auntie started coughing and it woke me up," she said to him. "I was about to go lay back down, but I saw you through the window."

She didn't look down at the bag so he was good. "Yeah, I'm waiting on Jess. She said she's running a few minutes late."

"Okay. I'll wait out here with you, bae."

Jessica pulled up a few minutes later. Nia got up first to go talk to her. Kevin waited until they were in a deep conversation before he got up. He walked up to her car and sat the bag in the back seat. They talked for a few before Nia walked to Kevin's side of the car and kissed him goodbye.

"See you tonight, boo!" she waved as they drove off.

Jessica was about to make some small talk as they drove away, but then she noticed the bag sitting in the back seat. "Is that extra equipment or something?"

"Nah, just 'bout to do a favor for one of my homeboys," he said quickly.

He was hoping to leave it at that, but Jessica continued to question him. "Umm, what kind of favor? That's a big bag."

"Look, this dude I know, knows somebody who stay across the street from the studio. He told me to drop it off and pick up an envelope. That's it."

Jessica's face scrunched up in confusion. That confusion then showed anger. "What? What the hell is in it?"

Kevin shrugged his shoulders. "I'on know what's in it. He gave me five hunid, so I told him yeah."

She gave him the look a mother would give a child when they've done something stupid. "So, you told him yeah just because he gave you some money? It could be drugs in there or anything. If we get pulled over, I can go to jail."

"We ain't bout to get pulled over, Jess. Your ass drive too slow," he laughed.

"I can't believe you, Kevin," she said while shaking her head. She didn't find it funny at all.

He took notice to her frustration. "Damn, Jess, I'm sorry. I didn't know it was going to upset you like that. Listen, if I do this again, next time I'll just walk. The studio ain't too far."

She didn't respond to him. She kept quiet for the rest of the way. When they pulled up to the parking lot, she got out quickly and walked towards the studio.

"I'm about to drop this off," he shouted. "I'll be in there in a few."

She threw up a dismissive wave as she walked inside the building.

He felt bad by bringing it in her car, but he knew he had to go ahead and do it since Chris already paid him. He reached inside his pocket and pulled out the paper that had the instructions on it. It was the same house that he saw Slim at a few weeks ago.

On the paper, Chris wrote down instructions telling him to not go to the front of the house. There was a car on the side of the house. All he had to do was put the bag inside of the trunk and open the back door to get the envelope that was under the seat.

He looked around to make sure no one was watching and then he completed the task. It took him less than a minute. He put the envelope in his pocket and jogged back over to the studio. When he went inside, Jessica was sitting in the chair. She rolled her eyes when he walked by her. He had already apologized and he didn't know what else to say.

They both were silent for a while, and after feeling awkward, she finally said something. "Kevin, we've been cool for a long time but you better not bring anything like that in my car again or I will be done with you."

"I won't try you like that again, Jess," he said with his head lowered. "My bad, for real."

As the day progressed, things got back to normal. They worked together on the project. After they left, she dropped him off and drove away. He walked over to Chris's house to give him the envelope. Chris opened the door and invited him in.

Henry was sitting on the couch playing a video game. "Cut that off cuz and let me holla at Kev," Chis said to Henry.

Henry slammed the controller down and cut the T.V. off. "Damn, why can't I ever get in on anything?" He rolled his eyes and pouted.

Chris gave him a look. "Man, yo young ass better go to the back like I said." Chris's voice got deeper as he gave Henry the command.

"This nigga only nineteen and he want to sell some dope," Chris said to Kevin. "His momma died a couple years ago and I shoulda let his ass stay in Georgia with his punk ass pops. He's not built for this shit."

Kevin swung his arms up. "Man, tell you the truth, I don't know a lot about the drug game either. This was my first time ever doing something like that."

Chris laughed. "Kev, I brought you in because you're smart. I can see it. You know how to handle shit. Henry got a quick temper and would probably fuck everything up."

As they talked, Chris told him about Antonio and how the cartel was ran. Kevin wanted in. He didn't care about the risks. He only looked at the *good* side of things. He saw how they were dressed, and how much money they had.

"I got a bunch of young pushers under me, and I report to the big man," Chris bragged. "If you stick with me, I will give you all the easy shit. Just like I gave Slim. Slim was a thieving ass nigga, though. He would come back with opened envelopes and shit. My motto is, you stay loyal to me, and I stay loyal to you. So, you down or what?"

Kevin nodded without giving it much thought. "I'm down. I just need to get a set of wheels. My homegirl ain't gonna let me carry it in her car no more."

"Shit, you could walk to the studio," Chris advised. "Matter of fact, I got a bunch of houses up and down that way that I serve. If you do that for a couple of weeks, hell, I'll buy you a whip myself."

"Word?"

"Hell yeah, cuz. And once you get the car, then you can take all of Slim's routes. We'll let his thieving ass suffer."

"Bruh, that's a bet. I'm down with that."

Chris filled up another duffel bag and told Kevin to just take a little bit at a time since he would now be walking to class.

After Kevin left, Chris went outside to smoke. Henry heard the whole conversation. He picked up his cell phone and called Slim. "Yo, we need to talk."

CHAPTER SIX

Them or Me

Just as Chris promised him, money started rolling in. Within a few weeks, he had enough to buy a car. It was an older Jaguar but was in excellent condition. He threw some dubs on it, repainted it and put some dark tint on the windows.

Before he went home to show it to Nia, he passed by Jessica's house. He decided to stop by to show it to her. They hadn't seen each other in the past few weeks because he wasn't going to the studio as much. Money with Chris was coming in so fast that he didn't have time for school. He felt that he knew everything that they were going to teach him anyway. Plus, he was getting his side hustle on by selling beats to Mike and others around the neighborhood.

When he got to Jessica's house, he walked up to the door and rang the bell. She opened it a few seconds later. Her eyes widened. "Hey, Kevin! Come on in." He walked in and took a seat on her couch. As she was shutting the door, she noticed the car outside. "I see you got a whip now, it's nice. You must be doing something good." She put emphasis on the word, something.

"I am doing *something*, and yes, it's legit. I'm selling these beats and Mike paying me for engineering at the studio."

"Great!" she replied cheerfully. "I'll be back in a few minutes." She got up and walked to her room. When she came back, she had on a change of clothes.

"You headed somewhere?" he asked.

"Yes, to class; somewhere where you haven't been in a while."

He shrugged his shoulders. "I actually thought about going today," he told her. They sent him a letter earlier in the week saying that he would be removed from the program if he didn't come back soon.

"Well, I can't tell you what to do, but I suggest that you come back. I'm trying to look out for you."

"I hear ya, Jess."

"And what does Nia think about all of this? About you not coming to class and stuff."

He grinned. "Nia don't know nothing yet, but when she sees that Jag, she gon' be aight."

She blew out her cheeks. "Uggh, Kevin, you know Nia ain't materialistic. She cares about your well-being. Listen, we start our three-week school break next week. At least come for the rest of this week and then decide what you want to do."

He looked at her and nodded. "Yeah, you're right. I'ma come."

He looked at the time. He needed to deliver two packages for Chris. "Listen, I gotta run cross town real quick and then stop by the house. Once I'm done, I will head to class."

"Alright, Kevin. If you say so." She didn't believe him. Kevin seemed lost to her. She knew there wasn't much she could do about it, though.

Kevin jogged to his car. He went to the trunk to make sure the product was there. "Shit!" he screamed. He left the bags at home. He panicked because he was unsure if he left them out in the open.

He hurried to the house. When he pulled up, he ran inside. Nia was in the kitchen, so he quietly went to the room to look for the bags. He couldn't find them. He walked to the living room and checked behind the couch and it wasn't there, either.

As he continued to search, Nia walked into the room with a bag of weed in her hand. She was upset. "Oh, is this what you looking for, Kevin?" She didn't say anything else. She waited on his response.

His mouth fell open. He knew there was no way out of it. Nia looked disgusted. She never would've thought that he would get involved in something like that. She tossed the bag at him. "You're lucky I saw this before my auntie did. She woulda kicked us both out," she screamed.

"It ain't like that, Nia," he said while locating the other bags. "I'm making easy money just dropping off a lil weed to different houses. I ain't doing nothing crazy."

"Kevin, this is serious. What if someone snitches on you? What if you get robbed?"

He remained confident. "None of that's gonna happen, I can promise you that."

Her eyes narrowed, further in disgust with his responses. "Boy, why would you think something stupid like that? You don't know what could happen."

His last defense was to show her the new car in hopes of getting her to calm down. He pointed to the window. "Look what I bought today with some of the money, bae."

She glanced at it and shook her head. "Kevin, I don't care about no stupid car or money. I'm here because I want to be with you."

"Look Nia, I've been putting in that work. I'm getting paid a couple hundred a day. I can't give this up. What you want me to do? Stay broke and live off you and your auntie forever? Damn."

"Kevin, don't catch no attitude with me. If you want to support me, then why aren't you looking for a real job."

He folded his arms. "How can I get a job? You know I'm in school."

She pulled out a letter from her pocket. "Kevin, not only did you leave the bags, you left this paper out. It's from the school. It clearly states that you haven't been to class in a while. How you gonna explain that?"

He grabbed the paper from her and started reading it as if he didn't already see it. He shook his head and sat the paper down. "Look, I can explain."

Nia walked back into the kitchen. Her eyes were watery. Kevin didn't follow her. He sat on the sofa and gathered his thoughts. Seeing Nia cry was hard for him, especially knowing that he was the cause of it. He started weighing the pros and cons. The money was good, but he didn't believe that it was worth more than love.

He thought about it for a little longer and decided that it was best to let Chris know that he couldn't do it anymore. He wasn't sure how he would react to it, but at this point he just wanted to make Nia happy.

He walked in the kitchen. He got close to her and hugged her from behind. "Baby, I'm sorry. I'ma call Chris later today and tell him I can't do this no more. It was a mistake, I guess I was just money hungry."

She accepted his apology. "Well, I need you to leave Mike and Frank alone, too. Auntie told you that all of them were trouble."

He took a deep breath. "Baby…Mike is the one who's buying most of my beats. You want me to stop doing business with him, too?"

She put her hand on her hip. "Umm, if I'm not mistaking, he's the one who introduced you to Chris in the first place, so yes, you need to stay away from all of them."

She could see that he was thinking about it. She folded her arms. "It's either them or me, Kevin."

Reality hit him when he heard those words. He didn't have to think about it no more. He loved her and wanted to be with her no matter what. "I choose you, baby," he reassured. "I'ma tell all of them that I'm done."

Before she could react to his response, her phone rang. Her eyes darted from side to side as she listened to the caller. She received some bad news about her aunt. Someone called and said that she collapsed at work and was rushed to the hospital. She told Kevin what happened and they both ran out of the house and hurried to the hospital.

*****

When they arrived, they were told to wait in the Waiting Room. A few minutes later, one of the nurses came out and explained to them that she had a severe heart attack and needed to undergo surgery to get her blood flowing again. Nia couldn't believe the news she was hearing. She was afraid that she was going to lose her aunt. Her eyes were flooded with tears. She leaned her head on Kevin's shoulder.

"She's gonna die," she blurted out.

Kevin wrapped his arms around her. He really didn't know what to say but felt the need to console her. "Let's just wait until the doctors tell us something. Hopefully she pulls through."

An hour passed and they still hadn't received an update. Nia looked at her watch. "What time does class start today, Kevin?"

That was the last thing on his mind. "It starts in an hour but I'm good, I'll wait here with you until we hear something."

"No, go ahead and go, I'll be fine. Once I hear from the doctor, I will call you."

"Alright." He got up and kissed her before leaving. "Call me once you hear something and I'll be right over here."

"Okay."

Chris called him when he was halfway to the school. He remembered that he never got around to deliver the packages. He didn't want to answer it, but Chris kept calling. He finally gave in.

"Yo, I got folks saying that you didn't drop off the goods yet? What's going on, cuz?"

Kevin froze up and didn't know what to say. He didn't have the courage at the moment to tell him the truth. He decided to just mention what happened with Nia's aunt. "Man, I was about to but I got a call from Nia. Her auntie is in the hospital and from what we hear, she not doing too good."

"Man, sorry to hear that and I hope she ok, but you still got a job to do. If it ain't done by this afternoon, I'ma owe them something."

Kevin drew in a deep breath. The longer he waited to say something, the harder it would be. He went ahead and said what he had to say. "Look Chris, I'm a man of my word, so I'ma do the delivery, but this is my last day working for you. Nia found out about it and it really hurt her. I need to focus on music and school."

"It's all good, cuz," Chris responded. "I tell you what, just swing by here real quick and I'll get one of the lil homies to take care of it."

Kevin looked at the time and saw that he had about thirty minutes before class started. He knew that he would be late if he dropped it off now, but he told him yeah just so he could get it over with. He also couldn't believe how calm Chris was about the situation.

When he got there, Henry came to door and let him in. Henry walked to the back and Kevin walked into the living room. Chris was sitting on the sofa. "What up, Kev?"

Kevin nodded. He handed Chris the bag. "It's all there, bruh."

Chris had a smile on his face. "Kev, I wanna show you something before you go."

"Sup?" He punched the air in frustration when Chris turned his head. He was hoping he could've gotten out of there quick and easy.

Chris walked to the coat closet and pulled out two duffel bags. He sat them on the sofa next to where Kevin was. He unzipped them and they were filled with money. "This is all the money for the month cuz. I gotta drop this money off to Antonio tonight. I'm getting a huge cut from this. You sure you don't want to ride?"

Kevin remained confident. "Man, like I said over the phone, I don't think that this is for me anymore."

Chris could see that Kevin was serious but that didn't stop him from trying. He took out a stack of cash and handed it to him. It was ten thousand dollars. "Look, Antonio gives me at least ten percent profit after every delivery. This is all yours no matter what... But, if you come with me tonight, I will give you another fifteen stacks, and I can promise you at least twenty a month."

Kevin stared at the money as he held it. It was very tempting. "Damn Chris, this a lotta dough, but I can't do it man."

Chris noticed the hesitation. "Cuz, this will be so easy. All we doing is dropping off the money to him. I just need you for the lookout since he's gonna give me another shipment. When me and Slim were cool, he used to do this run with me all the time."

Kevin's eyes widened. This seemed too good to be true. It was a lot of money just to go on a simple ride with him. "Why me then?"

"See Kev, I trust you. And I need you. You already know about Slim's bullshit; Mike trying to stay clean since his hands is around the music side. Frank... I don't fully trust him either. I used to date a girl named Katrina and he used to always say slick shit about her. I can't really trust him. But as far as the run, it's simple. I paid my pushers already so whatever Antonio gives me, is mine. I don't mind splitting shit with you if you're down."

Kevin didn't really want to do it but at the same time, he really wanted the money. There was no way that Nia would know that he was still involved if he was just doing this one thing. Also, with a large payday like that, he didn't think Nia would trip at all.

"Man, if it's gonna be that easy, then I guess I can do it. Do I still need to hit those routes?"

"Nope. I'll let the lil homies take care of that shit. Come do this deal with me tonight, and I will put you on some inside shit. I'll think of something."

Chris zipped the bags up and threw them back in the closet. "Kev, once I get off probation, I'ma buy me a house somewhere in Beverly Hills. I'ma look out for you too. Once you meet Antonio, you gonna be introduced to the inside operations."

"No doubt." Kevin then asked about Slim. "So, you mentioned that you and Slim were real tight at one point; how long have y'all known each other?"

"Man, we go way back," Chris explained. "The Katrina girl I just mentioned is actually his sister. I met him about a year or two before I met her, though. Slim and I clicked at first. We had the same 'get money' attitude. I then introduced him to Antonio. We started making all kinds of money after that."

"So, what happened from there?"

"Slim started showing his true colors. He's always been a shady ass dude. He even put his sister in danger several times. He used to pay Katrina to go on dates with men, just to set them up. She would go to a random restaurant or a bar by herself and if the dude looked like he had money, she would text her bro and he would come up to the spot, catch em' in the parking lot and rob them. Sometimes, it was deeper than that. If they had 'big boy' money, she would date them for a while and get them to buy all kinds of stuff. Once she got the passwords and pin numbers, it was a wrap. Some of the dudes weren't even lucky enough to survive. Man, Slim and his sister were ruthless."

"Man, how the hell did you end up dating someone like that?"

Chris laughed. "Trina changed once I met her, and I didn't know about her past until after we broke up. One day, she said that she was tired of everything and everybody, so she packed up and moved to Philly. Nobody has heard from her since then. Not even Slim."

*****

After leaving Chris's house, he still planned on going to class. Now that he didn't have to run routes anymore, it would open up time for school. It would also be away to keep Nia and Jessica off his back.

On his way there, his phone rang. He looked down and saw it was Nia. He answered and all he could hear was her sobbing.

"Nia, what's wrong?" he asked her.

Nia cleared her throat and spoke in a soft tone. "Kevin, she's gone."

CHAPTER SEVEN

Katrina

Katrina felt good to be back on the West Coast. Her time in Philly was good at first, but she started getting involved in some of the same things that she left back in L.A. She didn't tell anyone that she came back in town, except her homegirl, Toya. She tried her best to leave the past behind her, including her family. Her father was in prison and her mom died a few years ago. The only family that she had left was her brother, but he was still caught up in the lifestyle that she wanted to get away from.

She found a job at a liquor store in Long Beach. She lived in Compton, so she had to drive back and forth to work every day. Years ago, she fell in love with the Long Beach area and wanted to move there. She needed to stack some money first.

One day after work, she drove home, preparing herself for another boring Friday night. When she arrived, there was a blue Impala parked in her driveway. Someone was sitting inside the car, so she honked her horn. "Hey, you are in my spot!" she yelled. The driver's door opened and a tall, dark-skinned man got out. She recognized him once he got closer.

"Nate? What the hell are you doing here?"

He walked up to her while smiling. "Damn Trina," he said, "you know you can't be calling me by my government name. Call me Slim like everybody else."

She frowned. "Well, I ain't everybody else, I'm your sister, and answer my question, why are you here? How did you find out where I live?"

He leaned against her car door. "Henry said that he saw you at the grocery store the other day. He followed you here."

"You're talking about Chris' cousin, Henry? The one from Atlanta?"

"Yup, he lives here now with Chris."

She had a disgusted look on her face. "Nate, I know you're not here just to say hey. You only come around when you want something. I've changed, I'm not getting myself involved in that type of life anymore."

He threw his hands up. "That's how you gon' treat ya big brother? Come on sis, we blood. Look at how you living, I know you wanna get paid at least one more time, right?"

"I don't want to do nothing but take my ass in the house, I'm 'tied."

He walked around to the passenger side and got in. The look on his face was the same look he always gave her when he wanted something. "Look Trina, I know you out the game, but I got one last thing I need you to do. I know a nigga who gonna be carrying five hundred thousand dollars cash tonight. He's a lil, soft nigga. All we gotta do is take that shit and be out. If he tries something, Kandy can handle his ass."

"Kandy? Y'all still together? I'm surprised she didn't leave you by now. She ain't as smart as I thought she was."

"Ahhh man, quit tripping. Kandy is smart. She's about to start school. I gotta get her out these streets."

Katrina turned her focus back on the money. She really didn't want to get involved in anything, but she was broke. She barely had money to put gas in the car. If she did it, it would only be a one-time thing. She had to let him know that up front.

"Nate, if I do this, I want half of it. After that, I'm out. I'll take that money and buy this condo in Long Beach that I've been wanting to get."

He smacked his teeth. "Man, I can't give you half. I gotta pay Henry and Kandy, too."

"Henry? Why is he going?"

"Girl, Henry been putting in work, he part of the crew now."

"Well, what about Chris?" she asked. "Is he coming?"

Slim didn't want to tell her that the robbery was involving Chris. He knew that she wouldn't be down for that since they dated back in the day. He was going to set it up to where they wouldn't have to see Chris at all. The plan was to catch Kevin when he was alone with the bags. He and Henry came up with a plan to make it happen. In the meantime, he needed to let Katrina know that he and Chris weren't cool anymore.

"Nah, that nigga stopped fooling with me after he accused me of taking a few dollars from him."

Katrina frowned. "What? What you mean? Y'all were boys for life."

"Yeah, we were, but niggas change on ya' quick. He worrying about me taking a few dollars when he 'round here giving shit away. It's fucked up."

Katrina yawned. She was normally well into her evening nap by now. "Alright, Nate—or should I say Slim, I need to lay down for at least an hour. What time is this going down?"

"Meet me at my crib around nine, and we're taking your car because they know mine."

Katrina went in the house and took a quick shower before lying down. By the time she got comfortable, she was wide awake. It was a lot to think about. She wanted the money but didn't want to wake that part of her life up again. *I got to do this and be done for good,* she said to herself.

She knew once she got the money, she had to disappear again.

CHAPTER EIGHT

Back at the Hospital

Kevin arrived at the hospital about twenty minutes after hearing the bad news from Nia. He hurried into the building and saw her sitting by herself in the waiting area. He sat beside her and comforted her. Her face was covered with streaks of dried up tears. Someone from the hospital's staff walked over to them and had Nia sign a few papers. She walked Kevin into the room where they put her aunt and they said their last goodbyes.

Once home, Nia walked to her aunt's room and looked inside. She closed her eyes and tried to bring herself to the realization that she was gone. After she opened her eyes, she closed the door and walked towards the kitchen. Before she reached it, she felt weak and fell to her knees. She stayed there and prayed.

Kevin saw her and knelt down with her. "I hope it's not too early for me to say this, but it's gonna be okay, Nia."

"Kevin, there is a lot of other things to consider besides being okay. I am gonna to miss my aunt of course, but I don't know what to do as far as handling her finances. I believe the house is in her name, but I don't know. I don't know how to pay her light bill or anything."

"Look, don't worry about any of that. We will be able to handling everything." He was referring to him still working with Chris.

They went from the hallway to their bedroom. Both of them climbed in the bed. She laid her head on his chest. Within a few minutes, they both fell asleep. A little while later, Kevin was awakened by a text message from Chris. He wanted Kevin to call him. He slowly got up without disturbing Nia and went into the kitchen to call him.

"Got a change of plans," Chris said as he answered. "We need to meet now."

Kevin looked over at Nia. She was in a deep sleep. "Are we gonna be back a little earlier than planned?" he asked.

"Hopefully so, cuz. One of Antonio's homeboys sent me a text and told me to meet him at this new spot in Skid Row. I'm about to walk out the house now, let's go."

Chris was pumped up but Kevin wasn't so sure about it. He had too much on his mind at the moment. It was too late to back out of it now, though.

He took another a peek at Nia. She was still asleep. He tip-toed to the closet and quietly put on some clothes. He glanced at her one more time before leaving the house.

*****

Chris was waiting outside by the time he walked up. "You ready?" he asked. "It's gonna be quick and simple."

He rolled his shoulders. "Let's do this."

The more confident he tried to act, the more nervous he became. Kevin dealt with anxiety since he was a kid and now it was starting to creep back in.

"Wait in the car," Chris said to him. Chris ran back inside the house to get the bags of money. Kevin got in the car and waited for him. He checked his phone to make sure he didn't have any missed calls or texts from Nia.

As he waited, a car drove by, slowly. The car's windows were tinted, but he was still able to see that there were two women in the car. They both looked over at him as they drove by, then stopped a few feet ahead of him. Once Chris walked outside, they sped off.

"You good, cuz?" Chris asked while noticing Kevin's behavior. "Nigga, you look paranoid as fuck."

He turned his head towards Chris. "Man, I don't know. I saw two chicks roll past me in a white Caddy. They sped off once you came outside."

"Yeah, I did see a white caddy speed by when I came outside," Chris said, resting his hand on his chin. He then waved it off. "Ahh man, probably looking for that party by the school. Were they fine, cuz?" he joked.

"I ain't get a good look at 'em but you know I ain't stuttin' them anyway."

Chris laughed. "Yeah, I forgot, ya girl got yo ass on lock. That's what's up, though."

They pulled off and headed towards the meeting spot. When he turned down the next street, Chris spotted the white Cadillac parked in front of someone's house. "See I told you cuz; them females were looking for somebody else's house."

As soon as Kevin's car was out of sight, the white Caddy pulled out into the street and made a U-turn back to Chris's house. Henry was outside waiting on them.

CHAPTER NINE

A Deadly Exchange

Katrina drove past the black Jaguar and looked directly at the driver sitting in the car. She stopped a few feet in front of him and idled. Kandy was sitting next to her in the passenger's seat and Slim was ducking down in the backseat. Katrina turned her head around to him. "Nate, is that him?"

He rose slightly. "Yeah, that's him, now drive off before he gets nervous and think something is up."

Katrina slowly drove away. She saw Chris coming out of the house with two bags in his hands. Her eyes widened in shock. "Nate, what is Chris doing out here? I thought you said that we were meeting Henry?"

"Shit!" Nate said as he looked up and saw Chris. "Just drive off before he figures out we're out here."

She sped off. When she got to the corner, she made a right turn and parked in front of a random house.

She was confused. "You wanna tell me what the fuck is going on?" she yelled. "Why didn't you want Chris to see us?"

Slim sat up in the seat. "Trina, just pull up to where you see all those other cars at. I think a party is going on or something. We need to blend in. I don't want them to drive by and spot us. I need a minute to think this though."

Nate knew that he had to let her know something. "Look Trina, if I woulda told you that Chris was involved, I knew you wouldn't be down for it. But don't worry, he ain't gonna be the one carrying the bags to the back. It's gonna be that other nigga you just saw in the Jag."

Katrina still didn't understand nor believe him. "So, why is Henry coming with us? Does he know the details?"

"Yes, Trina," he replied. "Look, Chris cut everybody off when he met this nigga. Dude's name is Kevin. Chris got this nigga on a pedestal or some shit. All I want to do is get the money. Chris ain't gonna get hurt at all because he's gonna be sitting in the car. I sent him a text acting like I was one of Antonio's men and told him to send Kevin to the back to deliver the money. Henry's gonna have a mask on and is going to rob him when he walks through the alley. If he gives it up without a problem, then we good. But if he wanna act up, we'll have to put a hole in that muthafucka."

Kandy looked out of the window and spotted Kevin's car. "There they go right there," she said to them.

Once Kevin and Chris drove past, Nate was ready to execute the plan. He told Katrina to make a U-turn and drive back to Chris's house to pick up Henry. When they arrived, he was already outside waiting on them. Slim rolled down the window and dapped him up. "You ready to get paid, cuz?"

"Hell yeah, I'm ready," he grinned.

Slim got out the car and walked with Henry to his SUV. Since Chris knew what kind of car Henry drove, he told him to ride alone. He then gave Henry the directions to the building and specifically told him not to go on Alameda Street. Chris would definitely see him if he did.

Henry didn't catch everything Slim said to him. He was focused on getting paid and teaching his cousin a lesson for not believing that he was ready for the streets.

Slim also told him to wait ten minutes after they pulled off, but instead, he left right after Slim walked to the car.

Katrina was still upset. Even with Slim's plea; letting her know that things would work out, she remained skeptical of the situation. If things went south, and Chris found out that she was in on it, he would probably feel betrayed. Although they hadn't dated or even talked in a while, it didn't feel right doing anything behind his back.

*****

When they pulled up to the warehouse, she saw Kevin's car. She slowed down and got her brother's attention. "Nate, I only see one person in the car and I'on think it's Chris."

Nate leaned forward from the backseat and looked out the window. "Man, what the fuck," he pouted. Since Kevin was in the car, Chris was the one who was in the back with the bag. "Hurry up and speed off. Turn right at that stop sign."

"You think he saw us?" she asked.

"Nah, look like he was on the phone or something."

Once they got to the back, they saw Henry's SUV. Slim slammed his fist on the back of the seat. He jumped out and grilled Henry. "Man, didn't I tell yo' punk ass to wait until we left? Chris gonna know it's us, dumbass."

Henry kept a straight face. "Chris ain't a problem no more," he replied.

Katrina didn't hear Henry, but she did see the knife in his hand. "Somebody better let me know something," she demanded. "Henry what the fuck did you do?"

"I'm about to find out," Slim interrupted. "Trina, go park next to Henry's truck and let me sort this shit out." Kandy got out the car with Slim.

Once Katrina was on the other side, Slim got up in Henry's face. He grabbed him by his shirt and slammed him against the wall. "Nigga, who the fuck gave you the say so to kill him? I should smoke yo' bitch ass."

Slim was too strong for Henry. There was a height difference of at least five inches and well over a hundred-pound difference in weight. Henry had to keep his cool.

"I had to, Slim," he replied. "When he came through the alley, I thought he was Kevin. I pulled out my knife to rob him, but he had a pistol on him and made me take off my mask. Once he realized it was me, he asked me who sent me to do this. He then said he didn't give a fuck if we were fam or not. I took it as a threat so when he let his guard down, I stabbed him. He kept moving, trying to reach for his gun so I stabbed him until he stopped."

Henry's head turned to an area next to them. There was a dumpster and a small fence. Slim's eyes followed and he spotted Chris's lifeless body lying near the dumpster. He released his grip from Henry. "There ain't no way I can let Katrina see this shit," he said to him. "We gotta figure this shit out. And if Mike and Frank find out I had something to do with this, it's gonna be a war."

They were about to leave, but Slim only saw one bag of money. "Did you get both of them?" he asked Henry.

"Nah, I guess the other one still up there with Kev."

Slim paced back and forth, trying to come up with a plan. Even with Kevin siting in the car, it was too much light up there for them to sneak up on him. Slim came up with an idea. He walked over to Chris's body and pulled his phone out of his pocket.

"Check this out. I'm gonna text Kevin from Chris's phone and tell him to bring the other bag. When he walks through the alley, I want you to take it from him. Once you know the money is inside, kill his ass."

Henry put the mask back on and crept towards the alley as Slim texted Kevin. Slim told Kandy to wait on the other side of the dumpster just in case Kevin made it to the back. "Put a bullet in his ass if he comes back here," he said to her.

Kandy kept quiet for most of the night. She was afraid. After all of these years, she was finally starting to see how heartless Slim truly was.

*****

Henry called Slim to let him know that he got the bag from Kevin. Slim gave him the ok again to shoot him. After a minute or two, Slim heard the gunshots, but Henry never came to the back. Slim went around the side street to see what happened. He gave Kandy directions before going up front. "If anyone except me or Henry come back here, I want you to shoot they're ass."

Kandy remained in position with her gun drawn. About a minute later, she heard a noise coming from the alley and then Kevin appeared. He was looking around and stopped when he saw someone sitting in the white Cadillac. With his gun drawn, he walked towards the car. Kandy tried to get Katrina's attention but couldn't talk any louder without Kevin hearing her. Katrina had her down, so she didn't see nor hear Kandy. Kandy had no choice but to try and stop Kevin herself. She crept towards him. When she got close enough, she put the gun to the back of his head. She wasn't a killer. Her hands shook uncontrollably and she stuttered a command to him. "P-Put the gun down."

Slim appeared from the side of the building with the other bag in his hand. He dropped it once he saw the altercation with Kevin and Kandy. He noticed that Kandy had the pistol pointed at Kevin. "Shoot that muthafucka," he shouted.

Kandy turned her head when she heard Slim's voice. That gave Kevin an opportunity to react. He reached in and tried to take the gun from her. They wrestled and just before he overpowered her, a shot went off by accident. Kandy's grip slowly released from the gun and she fell.

Kevin stood there in complete shock for a second, but had to duck once he heard bullet's flying from Slim. He fired back and neither one of them were able to shoot the other. Once Slim ran out of bullets, he took off running towards Katrina's car, leaving the bag of money behind. He lucked up because the bag Henry had was right next to Katrina's car.

Slim's adrenaline was pumping and he could barely breathe. "Let's go!" he shouted at Katrina. She threw the car in drive and floored the gas pedal. As soon as she hit the corner, she saw the guy, Kevin, standing near Kandy.

"Nate, what the fuck happened?" she cried out. "Is she dead?"

"I'on know," he huffed. "I underestimated that muthafucka. He shot her and Henry."

"Well, let' go kill his ass and see if she's still alive," she demanded. "It's two of us versus him. How you gonna leave like that?"

"Look Trina, she's gone. The bullet hit her in her chest. Henry dead too. That nigga wasn't moving when I went up front. Now we *could* go back at get that other bag of money, though."

"Money?" she frowned. "Nate, these people are probably dead. Fuck that money! And whatever happened to Chris? I still didn't see him."

Slim gathered his thoughts. He had to make his story sound believable, and at the same time, come up with a plan. He was sure that Kevin would run off with the other bag of money. He needed Katrina's help to get it back.

"Look... Chris is dead. Kevin must've shot him before we came. We gonna make him pay for this shit. You and I can set his ass up. Do him just like we used to do them other niggas back in the day. You can flirt with him and make him feel comfortable for a hot minute. He never saw your face."

"I didn't get a good look at him, either."

"That ain't an issue at all. We'll ride by his hood tomorrow and I will show you what the nigga look like. If he not there, you will at least know where he stay. You already know what kinda car he drives. He shouldn't be hard to find with them short, raggedy ass dreads."

CHAPTER TEN

Confronted

Tremors shook Kevin's body. He raced down the street not knowing where to go; who to trust. He kept looking in his rearview mirror, hoping that he wasn't being followed.

He was completely blindsided by the attack and death of Chris. He knew that Chris and Slim had their differences, but would have never guessed that something like that would happen. On top of that, he was still in shock about shooting two people.

Kevin had never been exposed to gang violence in the past. In Florida, his parents were heavily involved in the church and did their best to keep him off the streets. He was an only child so that made it easier for them as well.

Now, Kevin was faced with a mess. The police could be looking for him, Slim could be looking for him, and even Mike and Frank. He pulled over to think it through. The one person who he could trust was Mike.

He gave him a call. He told Mike what happened. He just spilled it out all at once. Mike was high so he couldn't focus in on what Kevin was really saying. He kept telling him to slow down and talk normal, but Kevin was too amped up to relax. Mike then yelled for Frank to come to the phone. Frank grabbed the phone and put it on speaker mode. Kevin repeated everything that he told Mike.

"Man, that sounds like some bullshit," Frank said to Kevin. "I can't see Slim killing them. Even though they were beefing, Slim is still like family."

Frank pressed him but Kevin stuck to his story. "Listen, they got away in a white Cadillac."

"Did you get a good look at who was driving?" Frank asked.

"Nah, not really. It was some dark-skinned girl. I couldn't see her face but she did have long hair."

Frank tried to make sense of it. They knew Kandy wasn't the driver because Kevin said that she was dead. The only other female who Slim would take on a robbery was his sister, Katrina. "You think it was his sister?" he said to Mike.

"Katrina? Nah, I doubt it," he replied. "Last I heard, she was still in Philly. Plus, her and Chris used to date. I don't think she would help rob and kill him."

"I'on know," Frank replied. "It wouldn't surprise me if she did do some grimy shit like that, though."

Frank and Mike barely knew Katrina. They had only seen her once or twice and that was when she came over to Chris's house while they were dating. They probably wouldn't even be able to confirm that it was her if they saw her.

All fingers pointed to Kevin. Frank believed he was capping. "Look, just come by the crib so we can sort this shit out," Frank said to Kevin.

"Aight." He was smart enough to know not to go there. He just said something to get him off of the phone.

He was covered in blood and needed a change of clothes. Normally, he kept a few gym shirts in his back seat. He stuck his hand back there to reach for one. The first thing he touched was the bag of money that he had just put back there a few minutes ago. He had forgotten all about it.

He picked it up and pulled it to the front seat with him. As soon as he unzipped it, stacks of one-hundred dollar bills rushed out. "Oh shit!" he exclaimed. His fears and worries were gone for a moment and he was now smiling.

No one could tie him to the money except for Slim. Leaving the city sounded like his best option. First thing that he needed to do was to get Nia out of harm's way. If he didn't show up to Frank's house, he was sure that they would go over to Aunt Shirley's house looking for him.

He called her and she answered on the first ring. "Nia," he panted. "I need you to leave the house right now and meet me at the Fatburger by the hospital."

"Slow down, Kevin," she said trying to fully awake herself. "What hospital? And why do you sound like that?"

"Bae, I can't explain it over the phone. Just come on. The same hospital we were at earlier. Right off the 110."

She was still upset at him from earlier but could tell by the sound of his voice that something serious was going on. She quickly put on some clothes and left the house. It took her about twenty minutes to reach the location. She pulled up in the parking spot behind him and walked to his car.

His shirt was off and she looked behind her and saw it lying in the backseat. She picked it up but threw it down immediately when she saw the blood on it. "Kevin, what in the world is going on?" She said as anxiety and dismay filled her.

He tried to grab her hand, but she jerked away and frowned. "Don't touch me," she shouted. She knew that something had went down. He was too panicky.

He tried to ease into the explanation. He told her that he got robbed. Once she relaxed, he started telling her more. His intentions were to only tell her some of the story, but he spilled out everything.

She put her hand over head and sighed in frustration. "So, you mean to tell me you still hanging around those crazy ass people after me and auntie told you to stay away?" Nia was terrified, and also felt betrayed. She grabbed the door handle to get out and get back in her car, but he grabbed her arm.

"Wait, Nia. I was only doing it for the money. Chris offered me at least twenty grand a month to make a run with him. He promised me that it was no risk."

"Kevin, you are so fucking stupid!" she screamed. "No risk? Yeah, okay. He's dead, and from what you're telling me, others are too."

She put her head down again and exhaled harshly. The only thing that was stopping her from slapping the shit out of him was the fact that she was still under emotional stress.

He knew not to touch her, though. He stared at her until he had the courage to say something else. "What do you think we should do?" he asked.

She rolled her eyes and gave him a dirty look. "WE? No, this is on YOU. You're the one out here selling drugs and killing people, Kevin. You're gonna have to turn yourself in or something."

"I can't do that, Nia," he replied. "The first thing the cops gonna ask is why was I there in the first place."

"And you need to tell them. Come clean, Kevin. I would rather you get busted for tagging along than murder."

"You really think they're gonna believe that? Look, I shot two people. I could possibly blame it on Slim, but then I'll be a snitch and a liar. That shit ain't gonna fly with the hood. I got too much to lose."

"Well, you're about to lose me, Kevin. And what do you mean, fly with the hood? You're not even from here."

"It doesn't matter where I'm from, Nia. If I go down for this, I'm serving jail time right here in California. Niggas gonna know Slim. I'll be dead in no time."

"Well, you shoulda thought about that before."

Nia was tired of the excuses and bullshit. She felt it was best for her to leave town. Her aunt was dead and with him acting the way he was, there was nothing left in Cali for her. She could just go back and stay with her folks in Dallas for a while.

When she opened the door this time, Kevin was about to let her leave but he cut his eyes at the money again. "Nia, wait a min," he insisted. He pulled the bag back up to the front seat and showed it to her. "Look bae, we can have all of this to ourselves. I saw a condo out in Long Beach that's real nice. All I need to do is put fifty stacks down payment and it's ours. We'll be away from the street life and all. Plus, we don't have to worry about the cops because this is drug money. Ain't nobody gonna call them and tell them I took it."

"You can't be serious," she frowned while shaking her head. "First off, Long Beach ain't far enough to escape the city. Second of all, that's more than drug money. That's blood money."

"It's *Chris's* money. I'm sure he would rather me have it than them."

"Bye, Kevin." Nia shook her head and opened the car door. She cried all the way to her car. She had given Kevin her entire life and he wasn't willing to do the same. All he cared about was money.

Kevin tried one last time to convince her to stay. He ran to her car. She had the doors locked but she slightly rolled down her window, allowing just enough space for her to hear him clearly.

"Nia, we can build off of this money, bae. I promise that I'm done with the street life. I just want us to be happy. I can buy a bunch of studio equipment and take this music shit to a whole new level. Then legit money gonna be rolling in."

"Money, money, money," she replied. "That's all you're about now. Kevin, you put my life in danger by doing this. Here I was sleeping at home. What if they got to me before you called me? Seven years is a lot to throw down the drain but this is on you. You can live your life with whoever and where ever you want. Keep the money for yourself. Goodbye, Kevin."

She rolled her window up and drove off.

CHAPTER ELEVEN

A New Chapter

A few months later…

Kevin cut his dreads off and was now rocking a bald head. He grew a full beard and embraced it as the *new* him. He looked and acted like a new person. He was slimmer and even dressed different. Nia was long gone, and he was moving forward with his life.

He ended up purchasing the condo in Long Beach with the money he kept from that tragic night. He also rented a building nearby and turned it into a studio. He wanted a fresh start away from crime. He was making good, legit money now. He had no connections with any of the people from his past, including Jessica.

One day, after a long day in the studio, he decided to go to this newly opened lounge that was across the street from where he lived. The place was somewhat casual, so he went home and changed into a blazer and some jeans. He slipped on his shades and headed out.

Since it was just across the street from him, he decided to walk. That way he could drink as much as he wanted to and not have to worry about driving. It had been a long time since he had some alcohol so he was ready.

It was around six in the evening, so the bar was relaxed. There were a few people sitting at the tables and no one at the bar. He grabbed a seat at the end of the bar. The bartender hooked him up with a shot of tequila. He then went easy and got his next drink with a chaser.

As the liquor settled in, he started reminiscing on Nia. He kept himself busy during the past few months with music so he really didn't have time to think about her. Now that he had some peace and quiet, and liquor, she flooded his mind. "Lemme get one mo'," he said to the bartender.

Just before he took a sip, he smelled a sweet scent of perfume. He looked up and a young woman was standing next to him. She leaned up against the counter to the right of him.

She had a smooth, dark-skinned complexion and showed her pearly-white teeth as she smiled at him. Her eyebrows were perfectly arched and she wore a burgundy-colored lipstick. She had on a black bodycon dress that hugged her butt and hips. He glanced over at her a few times, but she had her eyes glued on her phone, still standing up.

"Excuse me is someone sitting here?" she asked.

"Nope," he said while smiling and pulling out the chair for her.

"Oh, thank you."

She was glued to her phone and her fingers were moving as if she was texting someone. Kevin didn't want to interrupt her but he felt like offering her a drink. She accepted and ordered a glass of wine.

Kevin wasn't dating anyone at the moment. His focus had been all on music. He was glad that he had some liquor in his system, otherwise he would've been too shy to conversate with her. "You're from here?" he asked.

"Well, kind of," she explained. "I was born and raised here but then I moved to Philly for a while. I recently came back about three months ago."

He nodded. "That's nice. I've never been to Philly, and I ain't from round here either. I'm a Florida boy."

"Florida... Hmm. I've never been but I heard that it was similar to Cali."

He smirked. "Nah, they're nothing alike in my opinion. Maybe if you compare Miami to L.A., but I'm from Jacksonville."

"Oh, that's where Lil' Duval from, right?"

"Yep."

He took another shot to try to keep the good feeling going. She showed a lot of interest in him and he did the same to her. She scooted a little closer to him. "So, what's your name?" he asked her.

"Oh, it's Katrina. What's yours?"

"Kevin."

She stared at him for about five seconds after he gave her his name but then she snapped out of it. He noticed it so he asked her about it. "You good? You stared off in space for a minute," he laughed.

"Oh yeah, I'm fine. This place is nice, right? I love the ambiance. I may come here more often."

Kevin noticed that she started acting a little different. She kept moving her head away when she talked and she avoided eye contact. She then took a deep breath and swallowed all of her wine. She shook off the rush.

"You sure everything good? You're not waiting on nobody or nothing, are you?" That's all he could think of to say.

"No, I'm fine. I just got a lot on my mind but thanks for asking."

He nodded. "So, you mentioned coming here more often. You live around here?"

She pointed to the building across the street. "Yep, right there on the eighth floor."

He looked over to where she was pointing. "Oh damn, that's where I live."

He was starting to feel that good vibe with her again. They talked about their condo and also talked about a few other things. Just as the conversation was getting good, her phone rang and she got up to take the call. When she came back, she had a sad look on her face.

"Sorry," she apologized. "I have to run, but it was nice meeting you."

"Nice meeting you too. I hope I can see you again soon, especially since we live so close to each other."

She smiled. "That would be nice."

She wrote her phone number down and walked out the bar. He watched her as she left out. He hoped that they could develop something in the near future.

CHAPTER TWELVE

Good News, Bad News

Jessica finally graduated and all seemed to be going good for her. She was introduced to a big-time music producer by the name of Kendrick Peterson, aka K.P. She was set to interview with him to become a recording engineer with his label.

After her graduation ceremony, she headed home. Despite all of her potential ventures, she still had to go to work. She knew that all her hard work would pay off one day so she didn't mind.

When she got home, a black BMW 750 was parked in front of her house. Someone was sitting inside who she didn't recognize. Since the car was in her driveway, she walked up to it and tapped on the front window. "Do, I know you or something?" Jessica asked the man. He was bald headed and had on dark shades. He didn't look familiar at all.

He took off his shades. "It's me, Jess. Damn, I look that different?"

Once she got a good look, she screamed in excitement. "Kevin! Oh my goodness, how are you!"

He stepped out of the car and wrapped his arms around her. "I'm good as can be, Jess. How you been?"

"I've been good. I see you doing well; new ride, new look, I like it."

"Yeah, the dreads were the old me, just trying to be different. I'm a businessman now, I got my own studio."

"That's awesome!" she gushed, "Come inside, let's chat; it's a lil nippy out here."

Jessica was so happy to see him. Over the past few months, she had missed him so much that she'd developed intimate feelings for him. She never felt this way about him in the past and she couldn't really explain why she felt that way now. Those feelings were growing even more now that he was in her presence again.

Kevin had a small box and an envelope in his hand. He gave it to her. Inside of the box was a gold necklace and inside of the envelope was a check for ten thousand dollars.

Him getting her the necklace had meaning behind it. When they first met, she used to wear a similar one all the time. Her mom gave it to her. She would normally take it off at work and sit it in her locker, but one day she forgot to put the lock back on and someone stole it. She was devastated. The necklace that Kevin gave her was the closest thing to it. He even brought a charm that was the shape of the letter, "G", which was her mother's first initial.

The money was a combination of thanks and a graduation gift. He knew that Jessica had always been there for him and she deserved it.

Kevin was supposed to graduate at the same time as her but he never went back to class the day Nia's aunt passed away. It didn't bother him though. He was satisfied with his life now. He had money coming in all the time.

She couldn't believe that all these good things were starting to happen in her life. She told him about her interview that was coming up with K.P. He was amazed and happy that she had the chance to work with a top-notch producer.

"Damn, that's neat," he said to her, "We need to celebrate soon. My condo has a rooftop restaurant that we can rent out."

"Cool, I would like that," she smiled.

They went from the kitchen to the living room and sat on the couch. She was about to sit next to him but decided to sit on the love seat across from him. She was trying her best to not show her feelings.

"So, I talked to Nia a few weeks ago," she informed him. "She's supposed to come visit soon." She brought up Nia's name just to get his reaction. She wanted to know if he was dating anyone.

"Oh really, I haven't talked to her since she left me. She doing alright?" He didn't give off too much emotion. His eyes were glued into his phone.

"Yeah, she's doing good. She got a new man and they ended up moving to Atlanta."

Kevin smirked. "Hmm. I was just there about three months ago and it's crazy because I saw a chick who looked just like her."

"Well, it's possible. She moved to a town called Woodstock."

"Damn, she was way up in the burbs, ha. Nah, that probably wasn't her. I was in Jonesboro with my partna, Zay."

Jessica picked up her cell phone. "Do you want me to call her and tell her that I got in touch with you?"

"Nah, you said she got a man now, so let her live her life."

He grabbed his phone and started texting someone. Jessica sat there and continued to admire his new look. She didn't know how to approach him, but she wanted to find a way to tell him her true feelings.

She took a deep breath and got ready to say whatever came out. "Kevin, there's something that I have to tell you."

He sat his phone down and looked at her. "Coo, what's up?"

She went over to the couch where he was sitting and grabbed his hand. She rubbed it slightly. "Listen, I don't know how this is gonna sound, but over the past few months I've been thinking about you a lot lately. Now that I've seen you, my feelings have—"

His phone rang.

"Hold on real quick, let me answer this." He picked up the phone. "Aye baby, what's up?" he said to the person on the other end.

Jessica frowned. "Baby?" she mumbled to herself.

Kevin told the person on the phone that he was just dropping a gift off at an old friend's house and would be leaving shortly. After he hung up, he turned his attention back to Jessica. "My bad, that was my girlfriend, Katrina."

She tried her best to not show her frustration, but it was getting to her so she let it out. "Girlfriend? Wow, you moved on from Nia pretty quick."

He shrugged. "I mean, didn't you just tell me that she did? I can't stay single forever."

She rolled her eyes. "I guess."

He squinted his eyes at her. "Damn, you sound a lil tense now? You ok?"

"Yeah, I'm good," she said quickly.

"What were you about to say before my phone rang?"

"Nothing Kevin. It wasn't that important." She got up and walked to the kitchen. She was glad that he interrupted her before she finished saying what she was going to say. Her feelings for him were strong and she wasn't prepared for rejection.

He was so caught up on getting back to Katrina that he didn't notice her frustration. He stood up and stretched.

"Hey listen, I gotta run, but let's do something soon. I wanna throw you a party at that restaurant. It can be to celebrate your graduation and your upcoming job with K.P. You're talented so I know he's gonna hire you."

She shrugged her shoulders. "That's fine, Kevin."

He still didn't notice her demeanor. He kissed her on the cheek before leaving. "See you later, homie."

Her feelings were crushed but she knew that she had to get over it soon if she wanted to remain his friend.

CHAPTER THIRTEEN

Uninvited Guests

Kevin rented out the rooftop restaurant for Jessica and was excited that she could finally meet Katrina. He invited Katrina's friend, Toya, and some new people that he had met in the past few months. He arrived early to get some things set up. He then called Katrina to see what time she would be there. She told him that she would be a little late.

Her problem was that she had some jealousy from the fact that he and Jessica were so close. She hadn't met Jessica yet but saw a picture of her. She also overheard a conversation while he was on the phone with her and she felt that he was laughing too much with her. Her solution was to go to the mall and find a sexy dress in hopes that Kevin would pay more attention to her than to Jessica.

Kevin brought the cake up to the patio and helped his friend bring in the DJ equipment. Jessica arrived while he was talking to him. She had a very different look. He was used to seeing her with jeans and tennis shoes, but this time she looked stunning. Her hair was flat ironed and it swung down to her shoulders. She had on a white cocktail dress with high-heels. Her eyebrows were arched, and her makeup was smooth.

He hugged her and complimented her on her look. "Jessica, you look amazing. I never knew this glamourous girl was hiding behind jeans and tennis shoes all the time."

She laughed. "Thank you, Kevin."

She was over her desire to be with him. She accepted the fact that they would be no more than just friends.

"So, where is everyone?" she asked. "Is Katrina coming?"

"Katrina said that she'll be here in an hour or so. As far as the others, you know black folks always late. I shoulda told they ass five o'clock instead of eight."

As they waited on others to arrive, she sparked up a conversation. "So, I just want to let you know that I got hired by K.P. He's a real humble guy."

"Damn, I like that. You're about to start making the big bucks now, I see."

"Probably so, but I'm more thrilled about the experience. I can't wait to get started."

"Well, let's get something to drink," he declared. "What do you want?"

She couldn't decide. "I don't know, a glass of wine or something."

He pulled out a stack of cash. "Girl, it ain't gonna be no glasses of nothing ova here; we poppin' bottles."

He called the waitress over and ordered a bottle of champagne and a few bottles of liquor. Guests started rolling in soon after.

Katrina arrived about an hour later. She spotted Kevin and Jessica sitting next to each other at a table. She walked over and stood right in front of them. "Hey boo, sorry I'm late. Had to run to the mall and then went to the house to change." Her smile was forced. She hated seeing them so close and comfortable with each other.

Kevin stood up and kissed her. He introduced them in the simplest way possible. "Katrina, this is Jessica; and Jessica this is Katrina."

Katrina's stare was long and disturbing. Once she saw that Jessica wasn't going to say anything, she extended her hand and shook hers.

Katrina now looked at her dress. "I see we dress alike," she smiled. "I got mine from Rodeo Drive, but I did see one like yours at that knock-off department store on Century."

Jessica rolled her eyes. She didn't want to say anything and ruin her celebration, so she walked away. "Kevin, I'm about to run to the restroom, I'll be back in a minute."

She walked in between Kevin and Katrina and rolled her eyes again as she passed.

"What is her problem?" Katrina asked.

Kevin shrugged. "I don't know, she probably didn't like your comment about her dress."

"Well, I'm just saying, it does look cheap, and why was she all close to you? Then when I came, she scooted over."

"Trina listen, Jess is cool. You don't have to feel like she's a threat. I'm not sleeping with her. It ain't nothing like that."

"Oh, I don't feel threatened at all," she snapped. "But y'all must've fucked in the past or something. I saw how she looked at me, she must be the one who feels threatened."

"Come on, Katrina. We've just been cool for a long ass time. Ain't nothing going on, I swear."

She finally relaxed. Kevin wasn't like any of the guys that she dated in the past and she knew that. She just never been with anyone who had close female friends. She told herself to chill and have a good time.

"Kevin, I'm sorry," she apologized. "You ain't nothing like them niggas I used to mess with. I just have to learn to trust you."

"One thing that I am is faithful. I don't have a reason to cheat. Plus, I'll be stupid as hell to cheat on someone as fine as you."

She smiled. Just before she said anything else, her homegirl, Toya came up. She knew that it was going to be a good time then. They had been friends for a long time.

"I'll be back, I'ma go holla at my girl," she said to Kevin.

"Aight, boo."

Jessica was walking back as she was heading to Toya. "Hey, I just want to say that I'm sorry for acting like that a few minutes ago," Katrina said to Jessica. "I hope that tonight you have a great time. And congrats on your graduation."

"Thanks girl. And it's cool. I'm just glad that you came."

Kevin was still sitting down when Jessica came back to the table. This time, she sat across from him to avoid any tension.

"She turned into a whole new person since I came back from the restroom. Hopefully she can stay that way."

He nodded. "Yeah, I think she will. At first, she thought that you and I had something going on."

She could tell that Kevin really cared for Katrina but was a little concerned about how quick they were moving. "So, you like her, huh? How's her family? Have you met them?"

"Yeah, I like her a lot. She doesn't talk about her family much. She did mention that she had a brother, but that was about it. She's a closed in person."

"Well, just be careful. Make sure you get to know her before anything gets too serious."

"No doubt."

Kevin was looking towards the elevator and saw two men get off. They stopped by the bar area and looked around like they were looking for someone. Kevin took a harder look at them. Suddenly, his mouth dropped as if he had seen a ghost.

"Hey, are you ok?" Jessica asked when she saw his facial expression.

He kept his eyes forward. "What the hell are they doing here?"

She followed his eyes and saw who he was talking about. "Oh, Mike and Frank?" she asked. "I saw them the other day and they asked about you. I told them that you were throwing a party for me and I invited them."

She invited them not knowing anything about the death of Chris nor the fact that they were looking for him. "Did you not want them here?" she asked. "Is everything okay?"

"It will be, he replied. "Let me holla at them. Go grab some food or something, it'll only take a few minutes."

Once Jessica walked away, Frank saw her and that's when he turned and saw Kevin. He tapped Mike on the shoulder and they both started walking towards him.

Kevin had his strap and was prepared to do whatever he needed to defend himself. He pulled his shirt up so they could see it.

Frank grinned as he walked up on Kevin. "Kev, relax," he said to him. "We got straps too, but that's not what we're here for."

He looked at the both of them and then pulled his shirt back down. "Well, I'on know why y'all here but I'm telling you straight up that I-ain' have nothing to do with Chris's murder."

Frank gave him the side eye. "It's all good, Kev. We just wanna know why didn't you come by the crib that night. You coulda told us all this in person instead of hiding out for months."

Frank was getting closer into Kevin's personal space but Mike stepped in between them. "Kev, we got all that shit figured out and know what happened that night. But the only crazy thing about your story is that nobody found Henry's body. I know you said that you shot him."

Kevin lowered his head in disbelief. "I know for sure that I shot him. It was blood everywhere."

Frank grinned. "Kev, we know everything, cuz. We know the REAL reason why you were ducked off."

"And why is that?" Kevin asked.

Frank grinned. "Nigga, don't play dumb. We know that Slim didn't take both bags of money. Word on the street is that he's looking for you."

Kevin took a deep breath. Although he had new money on his own, most of the money from the bag that night was spent. He spent most of it on the down payment for his condo and for his studio. He had nothing to offer them if that's what they were there for.

"Frank, let me holla at Kev real quick," Mike said as he pulled Kevin to the side.

Mike put his hand on Kevin's shoulder and they started walking and talking. Mike didn't have a problem with Kevin. He understood what he did and wanted him to know that.

"Look cuz, we know that you were loyal to Chris. And as far as the money, don't worry about the other bag. It is what it is."

That still wasn't enough for Kevin. He didn't want them there, especially Frank. "So, what's the real reason that y'all came, Mike? I know it wasn't because of Jessica's party."

Mike laughed it off. "You're right, lil homie. Listen, Antonio wanna holla at 'cha. He never got a chance to meet you before and he got some business for you. He didn't tell us when and where, but it will be soon."

Kevin did not want to go back to that lifestyle. He had already lost one woman by being involved in drugs and he wasn't about to lose another. "Nah, I'm out for good, bruh. Tell Antonio no thanks."

Frank overheard him and stepped to him. "It ain't an option, homie. If Antonio wants something done, then it's gonna get done. It's out of our hands."

"Plus, he believes that you rolling with some foul people," Mike added. "He didn't say who's foul but he told us that it was someone close to you."

"Who, me? Man, all I do is stay to myself. Just me and my girl."

Kevin pointed to Katrina while they were talking. Both Frank and Mike turned around and put their eyes on her. "She looks familiar," Frank said. "What's her name?"

"Katrina. I doubt you know her, though. She just moved from Philly and she lives over here in Long Beach. I don't think she got any ties to Compton or Watts."

"Nah, I think Frank is right," Mike said to Kevin. "I've seen her before. Damn, I just don't know where."

Kevin was sure that they didn't know her so he called her over there. "Bae, come here real quick!" he shouted.

Katrina was with Toya but then she walked over to Kevin. About halfway there, she looked up and stopped almost immediately. She locked eyes with Frank. Frank stared at her and then looked down and stared at her necklace. Katrina turned around and hurried for the elevator.

"Hold up, Katrina!" he said to her as he ran behind her. When he finally caught up to her, he paused to catch his breath.

"Hey, is everything cool? Where are you going?"

The elevator opened and she walked in. "Sorry Kevin," she cried. "I got to go. I will explain it to you later."

After she went down, Kevin walked back over to Frank and Mike. He was embarrassed and confused about how Katrina left so suddenly. "Look man, y'all get at me whenever Antonio wants to meet up."

Mike was about to leave but Frank stopped him. Frank was still thinking about the incident then something dawned on him.

"Wait," he said to them. "I figured out where I know her from. That's Slim's sister, Katrina."

CHAPTER FOURTEEN

New Opportunity

Kevin met up with Jessica about a week later. She had just got back from New York for a business meeting with the record label. They were inside of Flipper's Grill in downtown Los Angeles. Jessica hadn't talked to him since that night but she did remember that Katrina left early.

"Hey, what happened to Katrina the other night? She left once Mike and Frank came up."

"Man, I don't know what happened to tell you the truth. She just ran off like she was scared or worried about something."

Jessica pressed her fingers to her lips in deep thought. "Hmm, do you think that it was somebody there who she knew?"

"Man, I don't know. Frank swore that he saw her before. She didn't want to come close to them; and before Frank left, he mentioned that Katrina may be Slim's sister."

Jessica still didn't know anything about the beef between all of them, so she was clueless. "So, what's wrong with that?"

Kevin let out an exhale. "I'll tell you everything one day, Jess. All I can say right now is that me and Slim ain't cool no more."

She sucked her teeth. "Kevin, we are friends. Best friends at that. Why do you keep stuff so secret? Just tell me what's going on."

He lowered his head and thought about it. He knew that she wasn't going to snitch on him. He filled her in on everything.

She took in what he was saying, but didn't believe that Katrina was tied to any of it. "So, if they got a good look at her on the night of my party, how are they still not sure that she's Slim sister?"

"From what they told me, they only saw Katrina once or twice before. Me personally, I don't think that it's the same Katrina. She told me that her brother's name was Nate. I'll ask her about it one day, but for now, until she shows me that she's plotting against me, I'ma keep things the way they are."

"Well, if you trust her, then just let it go," Jessica advised. "You already said that you don't really trust Frank nem' so maybe they're just lying."

Minutes later, Jessica saw Kevin motion his hand in a wave. She turned and around and saw Katrina standing at the restaurant's door. She turned back to Kevin. "Oh, I didn't know that she was coming."

"Yeah, she texted me earlier and I forgot to tell you. Y'all gonna be cool, right?"

"Yeah, sure. She apologized to me at my party. As long as she stays like that, we're good."

Katrina walked to the table. "Hey y'all, what's going on?" she greeted. She kissed Kevin and sat next to Jessica. "What's up, Jess? How are you?" She smiled and complimented her clothes.

They ordered their food and sat and talked for a while. Kevin was happy to see them getting along. During the meal, he got a call from one of his clients, wanting to record some music.

"Listen guys, I gotta run. My man Ron is up at the studio waiting for me."

Katrina frowned. "Aww, we were having such a good time."

"I know. Well, let's meet up for the fight tonight. I got my money on Floyd."

Jessica turned towards Katrina. "Hey, if you ain't busy, I'm about to go get my nails done. You can come if you want to."

Katrina's eyes sparked with excitement. "Sure, girl. I'm down with that."

"Alright, y'all. Let me run," Kevin said as he got up. He smiled on his way out of the restaurant. He was falling in love with Katrina. He was glad that those two were becoming cool with each other.

*****

When he arrived at the studio, Ron was already there waiting on him. They greeted and went straight to work. Ron dropped that fire as usual. He recorded two tracks. After he left, Kevin received a call from his homeboy, Zay, in Atlanta. Zay was the same guy who Kevin went to visit right after Nia left. While there, he taught Kevin some of the basics of building a studio.

Zay was originally from Atlanta but spent time in Los Angeles and Florida. He and Kevin met while they were in L.A.

"Aye, Kev, I got some good news, bruh." Zay had a deep southern accent and usually said bruh after everything.

"Oh, yeah?" Kevin replied. "What's up?"

"Man, I'm about to get my own studio in Buckhead, bruh bruh. I wanted to see if you're interested in running it with me. I got connections with all the major artists down here."

Kevin loved his studio in Los Angeles but an opportunity in Atlanta with major artists would put them over the top. It would also give him a chance to get away from Frank, Mike and Antonio.

"How soon we talking?"

"Real soon, bruh. One of my partners backed out on me at the last minute. I have a building that I'm buying but I gotta make a decision by the twenty-ninth."

Kevin looked at the calendar on the wall. "Damn, that's right around the corner."

"Yep, just let me know ASAP. Just know that if you come, I'm gonna look out for you. You'll be my number one producer."

"Aight. Fa' sho. I'll get at you soon."

The twenty-ninth was only days away. He knew that he could easily sell the condo. He was just renting the studio building, so he could break out of the lease.

After they hung up, he threw on his gray hoodie and turned his Lakers Fitty Cap to the back. He walked outside and sat on the stairs. He thought about everything. The only thing stopping him from saying yes was Katrina. He didn't want to leave her. They briefly spoke about moving in together but they never said anything about leaving California together. He didn't know what her reaction would be. The only way to find out, was to ask her.

CHAPTER FIFTEEN

Love and The Unexpected

Kevin picked up a shiny engagement ring for Katrina. He was going to ask Katrina to move to Atlanta with him, and if she said yes, then he would propose to her. He stopped by Jessica's house first to tell her the news. She first noticed the huge smile on his face. "So, what brings you 'round here?" she asked.

He took a seat on the sofa and leaned back. "I got some good news from my boy, Zay."

"Zay? The guy who owns the studio in Atlanta, right?"

"Yep. He's buying a huge studio from someone out there and looking to start a label real soon. I mean, this dude has worked with all types of major artists and he asked me to help him start it up. I have to act on it soon, though."

She nodded her head in agreement. "Kevin, as much as I would hate to see you go, I think that it would be a great opportunity for you. You said that you wanted to get away from Mike and Frank, well there you go."

He gave a half-smile. "Well, there is one more thing," he added. "I'm in love with Katrina and I want to ask her to come with me. I wanted to get your opinion on her since y'all have hung out a few times."

"Hmm. I think she's really nice and if you love her, then you should ask her and see."

He showed her the ring. "I want to ask her to come with me first, then I'ma ask her to be my wife. I ain't bout to be left looking stupid if she says that she doesn't wanna move."

Jessica's cheeks expanded into a smile. "Wow Kevin, she would love that. You shouldn't have nothing to worry about."

That gave him the confidence that he needed. He left Jessica's house a couple minutes later and head home. On his way there, Katrina called. "Hey, bae, where are you?" she asked him. "I went upstairs to your place and you weren't there."

"My bad, I stopped by the mall and then Jessica's. I'm headed home now."

"Ok. Do you want me to order us some food?"

"Nah, let's go out tonight," he said to her. "I want to make tonight special."

Her excitement showed in her voice. "Ok, that sounds good. That art gallery downtown is open late tonight. We can go there if you want. They're serving wine tonight."

"Cool. That sounds like a plan to me. I'll be home soon."

This was perfect. She had been raving about the art gallery for a while. All he had to do was show her a good time, and pop the question before the night was over.

Traffic was light so it didn't take long for him to get home. The gallery event started at nine and ended at midnight. It was already a little after ten so he rushed and got dressed. He put on a Polo shirt and some slacks. He wanted to be clean but keep it casual at the same time.

He then went downstairs to her unit and rang the bell. Katrina opened the door and Kevin couldn't take his eyes off of her. She had on some bright-red lipstick, her make-up was done, her hair was cut in a short style and she wore a black dress that hugged her figure. "How do I look?" she asked while smiling and extending her arms.

He slowly shook his head and smiled. "Girl, you look amazing. I love everything about you. I'm one lucky man."

"Well, I'ma miss my long hair but I just wanted to change my look. I had a dream about us that I'm going to have to tell you about later."

She grabbed her purse and they headed downstairs. Katrina hadn't smile this much in a while. As Kevin drove, she looked out the window and daydreamed. She seemed as if she was finally coming out of her shell.

"Kevin, there are some things that you don't know about me. I promise you that I will tell you everything when the time is right. I just hope that one day, we can get away from this place."

"That *one day* may come sooner than you think," he smiled.

"What do you mean?"

"Let's just enjoy these paintings and see where the night takes us."

She grabbed his hand. "Sounds good."

When they arrived at the art gallery, they slowly paced around and looked at all of the exhibits. Katrina had a couple glasses of wine and after that, the exhibit was near closing time. Time flew by and they had fun.

As they walked to the car, Kevin felt in his pocket to make sure that the ring was within reach. When he got to the car, he opened her door and stood in front of her. He didn't say anything; he just stared and smiled.

"What's up, boo?" she asked him as she sat down. Her feet were outside of the car, dangling in the air.

He squatted down to talk to her. "Katrina, I know it's only been six months since we started dating, but there's something that I want to ask you."

Her eyes crinkled. "Ask me anything, Kevin."

He looked around before talking, giving him time to prepare what he wanted to say. "Listen baby, I know you just got back to California last year, but how would you feel if I asked you to move out of the state with me?"

She smiled. "I would probably say yes. There's a lot of things that I need to get away from here."

It was at that moment he knew that she was the one for him. Tears glazed from the reflection of the moonlight. He grabbed her hand with his left hand and pulled out the ring with his right.

She gasped. "Kevin!" was the only word that she could get out.

"Katrina, I know we both have been through a lot in our lives, but all that matters now is that we have each other. I'm looking forward to the future and I see me living a better life and you are the person that I want to share that with, forever. Will you marry me?"

She reached down and gave him a hug. "Oh my God! Yes, Kevin I will!"

She started snapping pictures of the ring and then she called her friend Toya to tell her the good news.

Once he got back in the car, curiosity struck her. "So, why did you ask me about moving out of state?"

"Well, my partner has a studio in Atlanta and he wants me to help him run it. He's going to be working with all types of major rappers, singers and all."

"How soon?"

"Well, I need to be down there for the grand opening in three days. You can come later if you want."

"No, I want to come now," she insisted. "There's two rappers that I hope he works with. Jeezy and Pastor Troy. I love that ATL sound."

"What you know about that down-south music?"

"Umm, just because I'm a West Coast girl don't mean that I don't listen to all music. I like everybody. They are my favorite down-south artists. Common my favorite in the Midwest. Biggie and Nas in the north and I love every Cali rapper."

"Well, listen, we gonna try to work with as many as we can. We gonna have one of the biggest studios there and it's in one of the most popular areas."

"Well, I'm down, Kevin. Shit, I'm so down, we can leave tonight if you want."

He chuckled. "I mean, probably not tonight, but we can leave first thing tomorrow morning. It's gonna take damn near three days to get down there anyway. We can always come back and gather our belongings."

Kevin was excited that she wanted to come, but he did take notice to how eager she wanted to leave. He just figured that she was done with the bullshit here and ready to start a new journey.

Before they made it home, Kevin got a text from Mike.

We need to meet tonight.

CHAPTER SIXTEEN

Facing the Facts

Kevin initially disregarded the text that Mike sent him. He seriously considered to just leave for Atlanta that night. He knew it was probably involving meeting up with Antonio and he didn't want to.

Mike sent another text. He was still driving and Katrina was on the phone with Toya so she wasn't paying any attention.

Mike: *Aye, u get my text.*

Kevin: *Yeah, my bad. Drivin.*

Mike: *Coo. Antonio wanna meet up with ya tonight. He say he gotta a job for u that's simple. Guaranteed to be at least 10 stacks since it's last minute. Probably more.*

Kevin: A'ight. Let me drop my girl off and I'ma head ur way.

Kevin didn't want to get caught up in anything else but since Mike mentioned, "simple", and "10 stacks", he felt okay with it. Antonio was known to pay large amounts for small jobs. That's how he kept loyal people around him.

He promised himself that it was indeed the last job that he would do. He was going to take the money and leave for Atlanta. Ten stacks could definitely go a long way in Atlanta.

Katrina was sitting in the passenger's seat and finally noticed that he was on his phone a lot. "Who you texting?"

He didn't want to tell her the truth. "My homeboy, Zay. The one in Atlanta."

"Oh okay. Tell him we'll be on the way tomorrow!" she exclaimed. She seemed to be happy with everything. Kevin now had no doubts about her.

When they got home, he drove up to the garage but stopped on her floor. She looked at him. "Oh, I'ma stay with you tonight. You might as well go up to your floor."

"A'ight, but I'll be back. I gotta take care of some business real quick."

Her eyes crinkled and she sized him up. "This business can't wait, Kevin? How you gon' propose to me and then leave?"

"It'll be real quick. I promise."

"Whatever," she said while sucking her teeth. "Don't expect no booty tonight. I'ma be sleep. And I guess I'll stay at my place. Just text me when you get back."

He was still trying to talk but she got out of the car. She walked to his side and gave him a kiss. It was a short peck but she loved him too much to stay mad.

At Mike's studio

As soon as Kevin walked in, Frank and Mike immediately looked at each other. Kevin's eyebrows rose once he saw the look on their faces. "Is something wrong?" he asked.

Mike looked at Frank again. "You gonna tell him or you want me to?"

"Tell me what?" Kevin interrupted. "Da hell going on? Y'all told me that Antonio wants to see me."

"He does." Frank leaned back in the chair and put his elbow on the control board. "We'll go see Antonio in a minute, but look my nigga, I'm gonna be real with you. Katrina ain't who you think she is."

"Huh? What are you talking about?"

"Look, I connected a few dots but Antonio gonna have to explain it to you. I have my opinion on the shit but I know you ain't gonna listen to me. Antonio been around all of this shit longer than any of us so he'll let you know what's up."

Mike could tell that Kevin was upset and confused so he walked over to him. "I know this may come as a surprise for you, but we will get it all figured out by tonight."

Frank was ready to go, so he got up and put his jacket on. "All I'ma say is she's definitely connected with Slim."

That hit Kevin in is heart. He didn't know what to say or think. Truthfully, he still didn't believe it. The only thing he could do was get ready for what Antonio had for him.

Frank drove his own car and Mike rode with Kevin. He felt that he could talk to Mike more than he could to Frank. "Man, is this some bullshit that y'all making up?" Kevin asked.

Mike tittered. "Look, I know you don't know Antonio like that, but one thing that the man keeps is his word. He told us to bring you here because he wants you to know the truth about her. He also wants to give you the job details in person. Whatever he tells you is the truth."

It was still foreign to Kevin. Katrina was too good and too nice to be connected with someone as evil as Slim.

Antonio's club was on the beach. It was the most popular club in the area. Antonio took it over after running the previous owner, Lawrence, away.

They had to park on the far end of the parking lot. Mike told Kevin to wait in the car while he went to go talk to Frank.

After a few minutes, Frank walked up to Kevin. "It's time, you ready?"

"Yep." He was ready to find out what the small job was so he could do it, get paid and head to Atlanta.

He put his phone in his pocket and got out of the car. There was a bouncer at the door and Frank told him that they were there to see Antonio. The bouncer walked inside and came back out with a woman. She walked outside and addressed all of them but kept her focus on Kevin. "Follow me, guys."

The club was huge and crowded. There were two levels. She took them to a table upstairs where a Hispanic man was sitting by himself. He had on a dark colored suit and dark sunglasses.

The woman who walked them over whispered something into the man's ear. He then took off his sunglasses and stood up. He had a scar over his right eye. It appeared to be from a stab wound. He greeted Frank and Mike first then turned towards the woman again. "Luciana, take these two men to their table and get them whatever they like."

Mike started walking away with the young woman, but Frank leaned over to Kevin before he left. "Don't mess this up. Do whatever he tells you."

Kevin nodded.

The man put his hand on Kevin's shoulder. "Kevin, nice to meet you, have a seat." He shook Kevin's hand afterwards.

Once Kevin sat down, the man sat across from him and put his elbows on the table. He gave Kevin a silent stare for a few moments. To avoid awkward eye contact, Kevin looked around in other directions. To his left, he saw a few men with suits who appeared to be bodyguards.

"Relax Kevin," the man said to him once he saw how nervous he was. "Welcome to my club. I'm Antonio. It's time to celebrate."

He had the waitress bring them a drink. Kevin didn't drink his; he was just ready for business. "So, what's this about?" he asked. "I heard that it was urgent and involving some money."

Antonio chugged the liquor down his throat. "Ahh… Yes, this is both urgent and involving some serious money."

He pulled out a cigar. "Let me tell you a story, young man. I remember meeting a guy who was about your age at the time. I brought him to a place just like this, back when I owned a club downtown. He had two characteristics, getting paid and staying loyal. I trusted him with everything. I was ready to make him the biggest drug dealer in the area. Unfortunately, his life was cut short; and I think you know who I'm referring to."

Kevin folded his arms. He was a bit defensive. "Yeah, I know you are talking about Chris, but what you tryna say?"

Antonio let out a harsh laugh. "Kevin, you would be in a box if I even had the slightest thought that you were involved in the murder of Chris. He spoke very highly of you and I know that you were loyal to him in the short time that you worked for him."

Kevin calmly exhaled and relaxed. "Yeah, I was. Chris taught me a lot. It's messed up how they did him."

"Exactly," Antonio agreed. "I know Slim was involved in the murder, but another thing that I know is that Slim didn't leave with both bags of money."

Kevin's skin crawled. *Here we go again,* he thought to himself. He wasn't prepared to explain to him what he did with the money.

Antonio grinned. "Don't worry about the money, Kevin. I know that you kept it, and for what you went through that night, I don't hold it against you."

Antonio sat his cigar down. "I do have another job for you. This is a very important job and shouldn't take long at all. I will make it worth your while and give you half a million dollars."

Kevin's eyes widened and his breath quickened. Even though he couldn't think of a small job that would pay that kind of money, he didn't care. That was a huge amount of money. "Man, I'm down," he told Antonio. The *old* Kevin was slowly creeping back in.

Antonio kept his eyes on Kevin. "Kevin, I must warn you, this is a very easy job, but a hard one at the same time."

His forehead creased. "What cha' mean?"

"The line between friends and enemies is a very thin one. Who you thought was a close friend turned out to be your worst enemy. I hate to be the one to tell you this but Katrina, your girlfriend, is Slim's sister. She is only in your life because you have what they wanted; the other bag of money."

Kevin lowered his head and fear transformed his face. "I'm not sure about this, Antonio. I've been with Katrina for over six months now. If this was all about money, then why hasn't she confronted me yet? Better yet, I haven't seen Slim since I've been with Katrina. Clearly, he had opportunities to catch me if he wanted to."

"That's how they do it," Antonio explained. "Slim has been using his sister for years, to rob, and even kill people. Sometimes she does it herself, but most of the time she gets really intimate with the person for a long period of time. Once they're vulnerable, she takes everything. Rumor is, she was doing the same thing in Philly."

Kevin was numb. It was starting to make sense now. Chris mentioned Slim's sister, Katrina, He told Kevin how she got down. She was probably in on setting Chris up. It was still hard to sink in, because Chris described her as a ruthless person, but Kevin always saw her gentle side.

"How can you be so sure?" he asked. "And how does she know me? I met her at a bar. Are you trying to say that her coming up to the bar was a part of their plot?"

Antonio smiled again. "Let me ask you something; when Chris died that night did you see who was driving the white Cadillac?"

Kevin thought about it for a second. "No, that's the only person that I didn't see."

Antonio winked at him. "Bingo. I guarantee that she saw you. Trust me, Slim sent her to see how you were living. He's gonna attack you sooner or later; that's what he does. Whether it's six weeks from now or six months, it's coming."

"Antonio, I was getting ready to move to Atlanta with her. Matter of fact, I just proposed to her tonight. Why would she do all of this just to set me up?"

Antonio shook his head. He was getting frustrated because Kevin was still in denial. "Kevin, she moved to Philly with a dude a while back. She met him here in Los Angeles and they were together for a while. That guy and several of his men are dead now. And look at Chris. She set him up to be killed."

"Well, one last thing, Antonio. She said that she only had one brother and his name was Nate. She didn't mention a Slim."

Antonio nodded. "Correct. She didn't lie. I'm sure you should've known that his ma didn't name him Slim. Nate is his real name. Nathaniel Jones if you want his full name."

As Kevin let it all sink in, Antonio showed Kevin a photo of Katrina and Chris. They were all hugged up, as if they were deeply in love at that time. "So, as you see, if she did this to Chris, she would definitely do this to you, Kevin."

He was now convinced and felt betrayed. He was boiling with anger. He wished he had paid attention to all of the signs. Katrina never talked about her past life and he had never met any of her family.

"What do you suggest I do now?"

Antonio put his hands together. "Well Kevin, that's where the half a million comes in at. I know that this will be a huge task for you, but you got to eliminate the problem and she is the key to all of this. If she's dead, then Slim has no details on our business. Trust me, he's trying to get info on what you are doing. That's probably why you're not dead yet. Matter of fact, I want you to take care of him too."

Kevin wasn't sure if he had the heart to do it. He had just proposed to her. He wouldn't be able to switch feelings that quick. "I need some time to think about this, Antonio. I mean we live in the same building and we just got engaged. Even if she is foul, I have to think this over."

Antonio was not happy. He signaled for his bodyguards to come closer to the table. They all surrounded Kevin. "Let me tell you something. You have twenty-four hours to handle it or there will be consequences."

"Okay," he said fearfully. He had a lot of things come to his mind. He could just leave and go to Atlanta by himself; he could kill Katrina; or he could go and talk to her first. No matter what he decided to do, he had to make sure that Antonio at least thought that he was going to stand firm and kill her.

Antonio said one more thing. "Just so you know, I knew where you ran off to the first time. Frank and Mike may have just found you, but I've had people tracking you since you left. Don't try anything foolish, and if by chance you do, make sure that you leave the area for good. You better go far away. That's a nice thirteenth-floor unit that you have. Katrina has a nice one as well. I would hate to see her alive tomorrow. Trust me, I will find you."

"Shit," he mumbled.

Antonio knew too much about him for him to not complete the job. It was kill or be killed. He looked Antonio in his eyes and told him what he wanted to hear.

"Don't worry Antonio, I'll definitely handle it."

CHAPTER SEVENTEEN

Facing the Facts II

Katrina was upset that Kevin had to run off so quick. She paid attention to everything. She saw him texting someone and wondered who it really was. She then thought about the time that she saw those guys at Jessica's party. What was he doing with them? She didn't know them that well but knew that they looked familiar. She remembered them from back in the day when she was with Chris.

She was starting to feel nauseous, so she sat on the couch and turned on the TV. She got up and went to the bathroom a few minutes later. Just before she sat on the toilet, she saw the pregnancy test sitting on the counter that she bought the other day. Now was the perfect time to use it. She held it under her urine.

Before the results came, she heard a loud knock at the door. Kevin had a key, so she didn't think that it was him. She quickly got up from the toilet. She didn't get a chance to see the test results.

"Who is it?" she yelled.

"Me!" a deep voice yelled from the other side.

She didn't recognize the voice so she looked through the peephole and there was a man standing there with his back turned. "Turn around so I can see you or I am not opening the door," she warned.

He turned around and it was her brother, Nate. She unlatched the door and let him in. She was disgusted. "What are you doing here, and how did you find out where I stay at again?"

He didn't answer her question. He was clearly angry. "What the hell are you doing, Katrina? Yo' ass been missing for six months. I asked you to do one favor for me and now you living with this nigga?"

"Living with who?" she snapped. "I live by myself."

"Bullshit!" he screamed. "Henry told me that he saw you and that nigga walking out of the building together. It's a damn shame that I had to track you down. First, you took my money and second, you fucking the nigga you were supposed to kill."

It was a lot for her to register, but the first part she heard was Henry. "Henry's dead, ain't he?"

The front door slowly opened and she turned to see who it was. She looked as if she had seen a ghost. Henry was standing behind Slim. He stood there as if nothing ever happened to him. He had a grin on his face. "He shot me, but I lived. Next time I get the opportunity, I'ma get his ass."

She was surprised but turned back to Slim to address the other stuff. "Nate, that night you told me to do you one more favor and I told you that I would think about it. After I thought about it, I decided that I wanted to be out of the game for good. I got a new car, new number and new house because I didn't want to be a part of your lifestyle anymore."

Slim was confused. "So, if you're out of the game, how did you end up dating this dude? You had a change of heart of some shit? You sleeping with the enemy."

"You got it wrong, Nate. My dude lives upstairs in this same building. His name is Kevi—" she immediately paused. Her jaw dropped. She remembered that the guy's name from that night was Kevin too.

"Wait, you're not thinking that he's the same Kevin from that night, do you?"

Slim nodded. "Think? Girl I know it's him. All he did was cut his hair. You stayed in the car the whole time so you didn't get a good look at him."

"Nah, Nate. I met my Kevin at a bar across the street from here. We talked and took things further once I found out that he lives in the same building. This can't be the same guy. My Kevin isn't involved in drugs and stuff."

"Katrina, it is him. He took the other bag of money that night. That's why he living large and shit. Plus, I'm sure he has a motive. He probably plotting on me through you."

Katrina sat down on the sofa as everything was registering to her. Tears rolled down her face. "He just proposed to me. So, you 're telling me that all this shit is a lie?"

"That's how it's done in the streets," Slim told her. "You gotta take into consideration that Antonio is involved, too. See, if you wouldn't've been avoiding me, we coulda been killed this nigga."

Katrina was hurt. She trusted Kevin with her life and now she felt that he betrayed her. She still didn't want to believe it, but the facts did add up. As she sat there thinking about it, Slim sat next to her and put his arm around her shoulder. "Listen Trina, I know that Chris was your ex and everything, but after he got out on parole, he started acting different. He gave me less and less work. I admit that I took a few dimes here and there, but I felt like that money was owed to me. Chris was racking up and I was starving. And as far as Henry, he tried to learn the game but Chris never taught him. Once Kevin came in the picture, they were the only two who were getting paid."

He also explained what led up to the night of Chris's death, explaining to her that they thought that Kevin would be the one who brought the money to the back of the building. He kept his lie on how Chris was killed. He said that Kevin was the one who initiated gun fire and that he was responsible for Chris's death. Henry also backed the story.

Katrina didn't remember that Kevin was still in the car when they arrived that night or she would've known that her brother was lying. But after hearing all this, she was ready to get revenge. "So, he wants to kill me, huh? Well, he can't if I get his ass first."

Slim was worried. "I'm gonna stick around and take care of him."

"Nah, I got it. You act like I ain't never handled a nigga before. Kevin ain't from the streets. I'ma teach his ass a lesson. He fucked with the wrong one. As soon as he walks through this door, I'ma shoot his ass. No questions, no hesitation. He's about to meet the old Katrina."

Slim smiled. "Good, sis. Don't give this nigga no chances. Ion care how long y'all been together. If it was all fake, then it doesn't matter."

"Don't worry, I'll handle it."

Slim and Henry left. They waited down the street so they could remain low-key. They wanted to be close just in case something happened to Katrina.

Katrina was just fine, though. She cut all the lights out, grabbed her gun, and sat in the kitchen waiting for him to come back.

CHAPTER EIGHTEEN

The Encounter

"Give me a call when it's done," Frank said to Kevin as he walked away.

Kevin had a lot going through his mind. He thought about just packing up and going to Atlanta by himself, but then he would never know the truth. On the flip side, if he confronted Katrina and she turned out to be foul, he could kill her and take the money that Antonio would give him. In addition, what if Katrina wasn't plotting on him? *Where would we go from there?* He had a lot of questions, and no answers to any of them.

Mike rode back with Frank this time. Kevin waited until they left before he pulled off. He drove a few blocks and stopped at an empty parking lot to gather his thoughts. Truth was, he didn't have the guts to just walk in and shoot her. He cared for her too much. He decided that it was best to just go back to her house and confront her with it and see what she says. Antonio knew where he lived, so he knew he either had to kill her or they both had to leave town that same night. There were no other options. Nowhere to hide.

He feared that he was probably being watched so he got back on the freeway and headed home. When he got to the building, he drove up to her garage floor and saw her car parked near the front. After he parked, he made sure that he had his pistol. He took a deep breath and pumped himself up before getting out. He then walked to the main door that led to the condo units. Once he got inside of the building, he looked around to make sure no one was watching him, and then he pulled out his gun.

As he walked towards her door, his heart started pounding in his chest. It got worse after each step. He pulled the key out when he reached the door, but it was already halfway open. At that moment, he knew something wasn't right. He pushed it open just a tad bit and noticed that it was dark inside. "Katrina," he whispered.

She didn't answer.

His adrenaline was pumping so he quickly pushed the door open with his gun in his hand. He heard a noise so he knew someone was inside. Katrina always left lights on in the house, so why would it be dark now?

He yelled for her again. "Katrina, we need to talk! I know about you and Slim, so just come on out!"

He heard footsteps coming from the kitchen, but it was too dark to see anything. The light switch was several feet away from him so he started walking towards it. As soon as he took a couple of steps, he heard someone running towards him and before he could react, he was hit in the head with a hard object. He fell to the ground immediately. His gun fell out of his hand and slid a few feet from him.

Suddenly, the lights turned on and he felt a gun on the back of his head. He was able to slightly turn around and see that Katrina was the one holding the gun. Her eyes said it all. She had the look of a true killer.

CHAPTER NINETEEN

We Want Some Answers

Mike was watching TV while Frank gave some girls directions to the house. It had been over an hour since they'd heard from Kevin. Mike was thinking that either he didn't do it or Katrina got to him first. Once Frank got off the phone, he told Mike that the girls were down the street. He could see that Mike had something else on his mind. "Yo, you aight?" Frank asked.

"Man, I called Kevin a few times but 'heen pick up."

Frank wasn't worried. "Man, fuck that dude. If it wasn't for Antonio, I woulda killed him that night we saw him at the party."

Neither one of them knew where Kevin stayed. Mike's first thought was to call Jessica to get the address. He was about to step outside and call her, but as soon as he opened the door, the women who Frank called were standing outside. They walked in with bottles of liquor and one of the women touched Mike on the chin.

"Hey Daddy," she flirted.

Mike didn't pay them any attention. "Yo Frank, I'ma go outside and make this call."

He walked to the car and called Jessica. When she answered, loud music was playing in the background. It slowly faded as she walked outside of the session.

"Hey Mike, I'm in a studio session, what's up?"

"Jess, I need Kevin's address," he rushed. "I think he might be in some trouble."

She was about to give it to him but remembered that Kevin wasn't too thrilled about them anymore. "What kinda of trouble, Mike? He told me that y'all only came to the party to collect some money, so if you trying to get at him about that, then I'm not gonna help you."

"Look, we found out that Katrina and Slim are siblings. I could tell that it didn't sit right with Kev. He went back to her crib to confront her, but it's been a hot minute and we ain't heard from him."

Jessica was scared. "Oh my God, I remember him thinking that she was the same girl from the night that Chris was killed, but he wasn't sure."

"Well, we damn sho' know it was her now," he added. "I need his address. I need to make sure he's good."

Someone from the studio yelled for her to come back inside. "Look Mike, I gotta go but he lives in that same building where my party was. I think he lives on the thirteenth floor and Katrina lives on the eighth. 1306 is his unit number and hers is 804."

Before she hung up, she also gave him the address to Kevin's studio just in case he wasn't home. Mike thanked her and told her that he would keep her posted on what he found out.

When he went back in the house, Frank was sitting in between the two women. "Yo, Jessica gave me the address to Kevin's crib. We should go around there and check it out."

Frank jumped up. "Hell yeah, let's go." He looked at the women. "Sorry ladies, but we gonna have to get up with y'all another time. Gotta take care of some business."

Mike didn't understand why Frank's attitude changed so quickly. Just a minute ago, he was saying, "fuck Kevin," but now, he wanted to go see about him.

Frank went to the back and grabbed a shirt. When he came back, he walked up to Mike. "What else did she say?"

"She also gave me the address to his studio."

Frank rubbed his hands together. "Last time I saw him he told me that he kept a lot of shit stashed in his studio. I tell you what, I'ma go to his studio and you go to his crib."

CHAPTER TWENTY

Finding the Truth

Katrina kicked Kevin in the stomach as she cocked the pistol. Her eyes blazed with anger. "Give me one reason why I shouldn't empty out this clip on yo' ass."

Kevin laid on his stomach; his face closed in a grimace. He managed enough strength to turn around and look her in the eyes. He still didn't say anything.

She kicked him again. "Boy, you better start talking."

With the gun in his face, that gave him what he thought was confirmation that she was setting him up all along. "Why Trina?" he cried. "You mean to tell me that all of this was a lie?"

She swung her arms down as she didn't expect to hear that from him. "Kevin, what the hell are you talking about? You're the one who came in with a gun. I am defending myself."

He scooted to the wall and leaned his back on it. He was still in pain from the hit to the head. When he looked at her again, she showed no compassion. "Was any of this real to you?" he asked.

"Umm yes, it was real. It was real until my brother showed up at my house an hour ago and told me everything about you."

His eyes widened. "So, Slim is your brother. Why lie when I first asked you your brother's name? You told me that his name was Nate. You didn't mention that he went by Slim."

She put her right hand on her hip. "First of all, my brother's real name is Nate and that is what I call him. Second of all, he told me all about how Frank and Antonio want me dead and you are just using me to get at him. Once you get what you want, then you would kill me." She raised the gun back up to his face. "But that can't happen if I kill you first."

"Wait, we have to figure this out," he begged. He had a strange feeling about the situation. "This sounds like either a set up by someone else or just a coincidence."

She ignored him and moved closer. The gun was pressed up against his forehead. "Close your eyes, Kevin," she commanded. "I'm gonna get this over quick. I can't believe that I trusted you with everything. You don't deserve to live no more."

"I love you," he uttered. Katrina was unfazed. He felt that there was nothing else that he could do, so he just closed his eyes and awaited his fate.

After a few seconds, he felt the gun move away from his forehead. He slowly opened his eyes and saw Katrina walking away.

"Uggh, I can't!" she screamed. She lowered the gun and let her guard down. Kevin saw an opportunity to take the gun from her, so he jumped up quickly and wrestled it away. She fell to the ground and now he had the gun pointed at her. "Stay the hell down!" he ordered.

She stared him down. He could see the pain through her eyes. "You came here to shoot me, so do it."

She wasn't acting like someone who wanted him dead. "Why didn't you shoot me when you had the chance?" he asked. "And I didn't come here to shoot you. I came here to find out the truth."

"Kevin, I want to know the truth, also. My brother said that you wanted me dead so if that's what you came here to do, then do it."

Kevin scratched his head with a puzzled look on his face. "Alright, Trina. I had no intentions on doing any harm to you tonight. I came here thinking that is what you wanted to do to me. That's what Antonio told me."

"Kevin, that's not the case at all," she cried.

They had to come clean with each other. They both had been concealing their past and in order to move forward with their future, all had to be known. Katrina thought Kevin was just a successful businessman that had never been involved in crime. Kevin thought that Katrina just had a rough past but was free from all of it.

He sat down on the chair that was in the dining area and began telling his story first. "I started off by moving packages for Chris. I knew nothing about drugs or any of this shit. Slowly, he started teaching me everything. I tried to get out but he introduced me to a way to make some money without getting my hands dirty. Turns out, your brother found out about it and came up with a plan to rob us. I don't know how much you had to do with it, but Henry attacked me first and he admitted to killing Chris a few minutes earlier. I had no way of knowing that you were in the car that night until Antonio just told me. Before I could get close, the other girl came from behind and put the gun to my head."

She looked up towards the ceiling and replayed it in her head. "I didn't get a good look at you either. My brother told me to wait in the car and that's what I did."

Kevin was now starting to feel comfortable. Either Antonio was lying or really didn't know what he was talking about.

Since he was starting to believe what she was saying, he helped her up and she sat next to him on the sofa. He still had the gun in his hand and kept an eye on her just in case.

"So, how did all of this get started?" he asked. "I know that you had a relationship with Chris at one point so how did all this shit go down like this?"

She took a deep breath and began to explain her side of the story. "Kevin, I started off doing a lot of bad things with my brother. When Momma died, I looked at him as the head of the house. Dad was already gone. He talked me into helping him rob people, and unfortunately some didn't live. I grew tired of it. I started catching feelings for some of these guys. Next thing you know they're dead. Nate is really cold-hearted. I couldn't do it no more. I met

Chris and we dated for a while. He was humble and laid back at first, but when he started hanging with Nate more, things changed. He got more involved in the street life. I didn't mind the drug dealing, but the drive-bys and shoot outs were too much for me. I packed up and moved to Philly. Stayed there a few years and then had to come back. I don't really want to talk about that part, but shortly after I came back to L.A., Nate found where I stayed at. That same night, he had a plan to rob you and Chris."

"So, why did you agree to rob Chris?"

"I didn't," she countered. "He didn't tell me that Chris was involved until we got to the place. He said that some other guy, which turned out to be you, would bring the package to the back and that it would be a simple lick. Chris's cousin, Henry, had a bloody knife when we arrived. I didn't know whose blood it was. I never saw Chris's body and didn't find out that he died until Slim told me while we were in the car. He blamed everything on you and asked me to set you up. I told him that I would think about it, but I decided not to. I changed my phone number and moved here. That's when I met you by coincidence. I swear to God, that's the truth."

Kevin took in everything that she was saying and he believed her. It was possible that they could have met just by pure coincidence. The other issue was that he knew more people were involved and were probably plotting on them.

"I believe you," he confirmed. "I'm thinking that someone on the inside might've found out about my meeting with Antonio and they told Slim. That's probably why he came here."

She nodded. "It was Henry. I know you thought he was dead, but he didn't die that night."

Kevin was surprised. He remembered Frank mentioned to him that Henry's body wasn't found on the night that Chris was killed. It was hard to believe that he survived but he just had to go with it.

Katrina didn't want to take any more chances with any of them. Slim already came to her house unexpectantly so she knew he would probably come again that night.

"So, what do we do now?" she asked. "It's not safe here for either of us."

Kevin tapped his fingers on the arm of the sofa. "I say we leave for Atlanta now. Like right now. I don't want to take any chances with Antonio. He wanted to pay me to take you and Slim out, so I know I'm in a kill or be killed situation."

Katrina had a nervous look on her face because he didn't tell her this at first. "So, you would've killed me for the money?"

He looked at her and wrapped his arms around her. "Hell naw, I just didn't know if you were in on something, but now that we know the truth, it's just me and you."

She had a face of reassurance.

Before they could leave, he needed to make a stop at his studio to get his stash of cash. He didn't want to put Katrina in harm's way. "Look, I gotta take care of some things, so I want you to go to Toya's house and wait there on me. Don't tell her nothing."

"Kevin, why can't we just stick together? There's no telling what will happen if we split up. I am ready to leave now."

"That's gonna be too risky, baby. I just found out that Antonio had been scoping us out for a minute. He knows where we stay at and everything. I promise you; I'll be back for you in no time."

She didn't agree with it but told him okay. She went to the back and grabbed a few personal items. As she headed to the door, she hugged and kissed him one more time. "Come as quick as you can and be safe."

"I will," he replied. "And whatever you do, don't answer if your brother calls you. I got a feeling he's gonna try to contact you again tonight."

She showed him the gun as she put it in her purse. "He's the main reason why all of this shit happened anyway. I'll kill his ass before I let something happen to you."

CHAPTER TWENTY-ONE

When Fate Finds You

Kevin went upstairs to get a few things out of his unit before heading to the studio to pick up the cash. Something told him to put on the bullet-proof vest that he had. He had gotten it from Chris a while back. He just felt that something could go down and wanted to protect himself as best as possible.

As he left out, he realized that he didn't have his cell phone on him. He then remembered that he left it inside Katrina's place.

He wanted to leave as quick as he could. He hurried to the elevator and went to her unit. His phone was lying on the ground right where Katrina had knocked him down at earlier. When he picked it up, he saw several missed calls from Mike and Frank. He ignored them. There was no need to talk to them anymore since he was leaving for Atlanta that night.

Before leaving her house, he went to her bathroom to pee. While standing by the toilet, he saw a used pregnancy test lying on the floor. He picked it up. Before he could react, his phone rang. It was Jessica and she was frantic with worry.

"Kevin, oh my God! I'm glad to hear that you are safe."

He was unaware that Mike called her looking for him. "I'm good, me and Trina 'bout to head out of town, Jess. Why do you sound so ecstatic?"

She was glad that he was safe but was confused about everything. "Why are you leaving with her? Mike told me that Katrina was Slim's sister and they were plotting to kill you. Are you sure this is smart?"

"It's a long story and a huge misunderstanding. They are brother and sister but she's not in on anything. It's just a crazy ass coincidence. I'll definitely explain it to you later. For right now, I just need to get out of here."

"Yes, please get out of there now, Kevin," she warned. "I was so worried about you that I gave your address to Mike. They may be coming there. I don't know if you can trust them or not."

Kevin was already by the door, getting ready to walk out. As he opened the door, he was stopped dead in his tracks. Henry and Slim were standing there. They pushed their way inside.

Slim grinned. "Finally caught up with yo ass. You let cha guard down, homie."

Kevin didn't know what they were about to do so he tried to reason with them. "Look Slim, I just talked with Trina and we got this all sorted out. I'm done working for Antonio and we're trying to get away from all of this."

Jessica was still on the line and heard everything. She panicked but knew there was nothing that she could do now. Slim took the phone out of Kevin's hand. He put the gun to his face and forced him to sit down. He was there for other reasons. "I don't give a fuck about what you and Katrina doing. If she's dumb enough to stay with you, then that's her. All I want is my money."

The bag that Kevin had in his hand only had about five thousand dollars in it. The rest of his money was inside the studio. "Take what I have, bro. Just let me leave," he pleaded.

Henry took the bag from him and handed it over to Slim. Slim opened the bag and counted it. "Nigga, you took over two-hundred and fifty thousand from me, this ain't nothing."

Henry pulled out a gun as well. "Let me take care of this fool," he said to Slim.

"Nah, first he gonna let me know where the money at. If it's all there, I may let his ass live on the strength of my sister."

Kevin thanked him. He then told him the same story that he told Katrina about how they met. Slim listened carefully to him.

"You know, Kev that do sound like a helluva coincidence. You're not a street nigga, so I shoulda known you ain't have the nuts to try to set me up. Yeen bout that life. But none of that shit really matters. All I'm concerned about is the money. I know you got a stash somewhere."

Kevin wanted to get out of there so he told him the truth. "Alight, man. I got some money at my studio. I will follow y'all there and you can have it all. I just want to get back with Katrina so we can leave town."

"Nah. I'll take you. If the money there, I will bring you back here. Now let's go." Kevin walked out first and Slim and Henry followed. Henry was pointing the gun at his back and looked over at Slim. "You really gonna let this nigga live?"

Slim whispered to Henry. "I'll leave that up to you, Henry. After you get the money from inside his studio, you can do whatever you want to him."

Kevin heard him and knew that if it was up to Henry, he wouldn't survive. Kevin turned his head and saw that Henry had a pocketknife sticking out. He quickly reached and grabbed it. He stabbed Henry in the arm and tried to run but Slim was able to grab his shirt collar and pull him in. Kevin had some fight in him and they wrestled. Slim's gold chain fell off in the process. Slim used his size and strength to overpower Kevin.

"Help!" he shouted.

Henry hit him in the head and knocked him out. "Shut the hell up!" he commanded. "You definitely gonna die tonight."

They carried Kevin to Slim's truck and threw him in the backseat. Slim drove and Henry sat in the back with Kevin. He woke up once they left the unit. Henry held the gun to his head and ordered him to give them directions to his studio. It was near the corner of Tenth Street and Atlantic. When they arrived, Slim parked in the back and told Henry to get out and get the money. "I got to make a call so I need you to handle this for me and hurry up," Slim added.

Henry snatched Kevin out of the truck and they started walking to the building. "You shoulda took that money and left L.A."

Kevin didn't respond. He just kept walking. When they got to the front, Kevin realized that he didn't have the studio keys on him. "I need you to untie me."

"For what?" Henry asked.

"I ain't got my keys. We need to force the door open."

Henry laughed. "You must think I'm stupid. If I untie you, all you gonna do is try to run away."

"Listen," Kevin advised. "It's gonna take both of our strength to get the door opened without a key. One person needs to pull from the top and the person on the bottom can lift it up a little and it should open."

Henry didn't believe him, so he tried it himself. He pulled on it. "Fuck!" He couldn't get it open. He then walked over to Kevin and untied him. "I'ma pull from the top. Don't try nothing stupid," Henry warned.

Henry grabbed a chair to stand on. The strength of them together got it open. Just as Henry was about to come down, Kevin kicked the chair and Henry fell down hard. The back of his head hit the concrete and blood poured from the back of his head.

Kevin walked up to him. The fall split his head open. It only took seconds for him to die. Kevin stared at him until he took his last breath. He had to make sure that he was really dead this time.

He walked in the door of the studio and grabbed the cash out of the safe. He put it in a duffel bag and held it over his shoulder. When he stepped back out, he grabbed Henry's gun and headed to Slim's truck. Slim was still on the phone and thought it was Henry. Without looking towards him, he started talking.

"Nigga, I-ain' hear no gunshots. Did you get the bag?"

Kevin got closer so he could see him. "Get out the truck, Slim."

Slim got out but wasn't fazed at all. He had a smile on his face. "Kevin, you've grown some courage since you been with my sister, ha? Well, nigga I don't think you'll do it."

Kevin had a lot of adrenaline pumping but didn't pull the trigger. "You're right," he told Slim. "If I wanted you dead, I coulda snuck up on you and taken you out like I just did your partna over there."

"So, you killed him, ha?"

Kevin stayed silent. Slim nodded and smirked. He looked into Kevin's eyes and saw a face of determination. For once, Slim showed compassion. He knew Kevin had just got involved in the wrong lifestyle and was legitimately trying to get out.

"Kev, you win this round. If it's really legit with you and my sister, just take the bag and leave. We may cross paths again one day."

Kevin shook his head in disagreement. "Let's end this beef right here, Slim. Fuck all that *next round* talk. I love your sister to death and I will be with her no matter what. We don't need to be beefing like this. If it's all about money to you, then take it, bruh."

He tried to hand the bag over, but Slim refused it. Slim indeed loved his sister. He started thinking about all the crazy shit he put her through in her life. If she was happy with Kevin then he had to accept it. "Kevin, you actually alright with me. I guess my sister loves you and I respect that."

Kevin relaxed. Slim seemed sincere. "I just want to get out of here alive and go back to my woman. What happened has already happened. We can put this shit behind us."

They embraced. "No doubt, Kev. You want a ride?"

Kevin still didn't fully trust him enough to get back in the car with him. "Nah, I'm good Slim. I'll figure out something."

Slim got in his truck and drove off. Kevin watched him. Once he was out of sight, he walked towards the main road, in search of a payphone since his phone was still at Katrina's house. When he found one, he called Mike first. He no longer cared if they were after him. He wanted to clear the air with all of them. He was even willing to give the money back to them.

Mike was actually relieved to know that Kevin was okay but was also worried about the fact that Kevin was trying to get out of the game. "You gon' have to leave California if you think you can hide from Antonio."

"That's the plan. We leaving tonight."

"Well, leave now, cuz. Frank should be headed your way in a few minutes. It ain't no telling what he's up to."

Kevin punched the phone. "Dammit! How did he find the address to the studio?"

"Man, we thought that something happened to you so I called Jessica and talked her into giving us your studio address and home address. The plan was for Frank to go up to the studio looking for you and for me to go to your crib. I'm actually about five minutes from your house now."

Kevin wanted to get out of there before Frank arrived, but he didn't have a ride. He didn't want to call Katrina and risk someone following her. His only choice was to call Jessica. She was already distraught because of what she heard on the phone earlier.

The panic was in her voice. "Kevin! What happened?" she screamed. "I was still on the phone when they walked through the door. I heard a lot of commotion. I almost called the police."

"Girl, I'm Superman," he joked. "Been dodging bullets all damn night."

He assured her that he was ok. He told her that it was Henry and Slim who attacked him but it was all settled. He didn't tell her that he just killed Henry. He also asked her to come pick him up and take him to Toya's house to get Katrina.

"Ok Kev, give me about twenty minutes," she told him.

After they hung up, he walked to the other side of the building to wait on her. He didn't want to be spotted by Frank or even by Slim if he decided to come back. He took a seat on the bench. He started thinking about

Katrina. It had been a while since they talked so he knew that she was worried about him. He walked back to the other side of the building and used the payphone again.

As he picked up the payphone, there was a silver Lexus driving towards him from the main road. He had his back turned, so he didn't see it. Once he started dialing her number, he heard the car and turned around. The car was approaching slowly. He had never seen the car before, but he knew something was about happen.

The Lexus had dark tint and the driver slightly rolled down the window and pointed a gun at him. He couldn't see his face. He dropped the phone and picked up the bag and started running. The car gave chase and fired a couple of shots from the vehicle. One hit Kevin in the arm. As he continued to run, he was hit in the leg and fell. The driver got out of the vehicle and ran to him.

Kevin could feel the burn all over his body. He felt the guy approaching and all he could do was try to crawl away. The gunman then stepped on his back with his right foot and leaned down to take the bag of money from him. As Kevin turned around, he saw that the gunman had on a mask and a huge cut on his hand that looked fresh.

At first, he thought that it was Slim, but the guy was way too short. His second thought was that it was one of

Antonio's men coming to kill him since he didn't kill Katrina. He was scared. "Come on man, just take the money," he cried.

The gunman raised the gun back up to Kevin. "Nah, this the end of the road for you."

Kevin's eyes widened in terror. The man fired three shots and they all hit his chest area. He took the bag and ran back to his car.

Kevin was hurt bad. He felt that the end of his life was near. He started thinking about everything. From the first time his parents told him not to leave Florida, all the way to this moment and everything in between. He hoped that Katrina was ok. He loved her and was glad that they made peace.

The pain was starting to fade. He was too weak to move. Suddenly, he felt his body go completely numb. He laid there and looked up at the night sky for as long as he could. Through it all, he was somehow at peace. He stared at the sky a little longer and slowly closed his eyes.

CHAPTER TWENTY-TWO

Frank's Call to Mike

When Mike picked up the phone, he could hear Frank breathing heavily.

"Yo, Frank, you good?"

"I'm good, where you at?"

"I'm on Atlantic, just passed Sixth Street. I was around the corner from Kev's house and he called me. He's not home so I turned around. What's up?"

Frank paused for a moment. "Turn back around and meet me at his crib."

Mike made a quick U-turn. "Alright cool, was he at the studio?"

Frank didn't answer his question. "Just meet me on the eighth floor."

Frank hung up the phone. Mike knew something was up. Frank sounded different. He called the payphone where Kevin last called him and the line was busy. He then called Jessica. "Aye Jess, did Kev ever get in touch with you?"

She was hesitant to speak. "Yeah, why?"

"Frank went up there to the studio looking for him. I asked him did he see him and he didn't answer me. I just want to make sure he good."

"Look Mike, he's good. I really don't know what y'all are doing, but you need to stop calling me. I'm on my way to pick him up now. He shared his doubts about you, Frank, Antonio and Slim. I think he just don't want to be bothered with y'all."

"I respect that, Jess. I'm just glad that he good."

She then hung up the phone on him. By that time, Mike was pulling up to the garage. He parked on the eighth floor and sent Frank a text to let him know that he was there. Frank then called him. "I need you to go to unit eight-o-fo' and see if Katrina up there. I need to talk to her."

Mike didn't know why he wanted to talk to her, but he followed orders anyway. When he got to the unit, he noticed that the door was halfway open and there was some blood on the wall. Slim's chain was on the ground as well.

CHAPTER TWENTY-THREE

Revenge or Vengeance?

Katrina had no choice but to leave Toya's house and head back home. It had been over an hour since she heard anything from Kevin and she was very worried. She called his cell phone, but he didn't pick up.

When she arrived at the condo, she went to his unit first and he wasn't there. She went downstairs to her unit and saw that the door was halfway open and there was blood on the wall. She also saw her brother's gold chain in the hallway. She pulled out her gun from her purse and walked all the way inside. She heard a noise from the kitchen.

"Kevin, is that you?" she yelled.

She heard footsteps walking towards her. It was Mike.

"Put your fucking hands up!" she screamed as she pointed the gun at him.

He tried to explain who he was. "Wait, don't shoot! I'm Mike, a friend of Kevin's."

She sized him up. "I know who you are and you ain't no damn friend of his. I've seen you with my brother before and I also seen you with Chris. I knew you looked familiar when I saw you at Jessica's party."

Mike still had his hands raised. "Well, *I am* a friend of his. I only came here because Frank told me that he wanted to talk to you."

She looked around and saw more blood on the floor. She also saw Kevin's phone lying next to a gun. She stormed towards Mike. "You got some explaining to do. Where the hell is Kevin? I don't give a damn about Frank, Slim or none of y'all. I just want to know that my man is ok. I saw my brother's chain outside. It looks like a fight took place or something."

Katrina was ready to kill if she didn't get a good answer.

Mike stuttered a little. "I-I don't know, I just got here. When I talked to him, he said that he was catching a ride to you and that y'all were heading out of town."

Katrina wasn't buying it. "So, why the hell is my place looking like this? Why didn't he call me? His phone is in here. I'm sorry Mike but I ain't believing nothing you saying right now."

Mike didn't have any answers for her. He had just talked to Kevin so he didn't know what was going on nor did he know why Frank wanted him to come there. "Katrina, like I said before, Frank told me to meet him here. I swear I'on know what's going on. Did you try to call Jessica?"

"No, I didn't, but I will." She had a little faith that he was telling the truth. *Jessica better validate his story.* If not, he's done.

She grabbed her phone while still keeping an eye on Mike. She called Jessica and asked her some questions to try and piece everything together. Jessica had no knowledge that Kevin was just shot so she validated Mike's story. She told Katrina that she was heading to Kevin's studio to pick him up and take him to her. She also gave Katrina a run-down of events.

Katrina told Jessica that Mike was in her apartment and she didn't know why. Jessica said something that may have saved his life.

"I gave Mike your addresses when we were looking for Kevin. I honestly wanted to call you but they were convinced that you had something to do with Kevin being attacked."

Katrina understood. "It's ok, girl. I told my brother that I would handle it, but it looks like he took matters into his own hands. I'm just glad that nothing happened to Kevin."

"Yeah, he's okay. I'm a few minutes from him."

"Okay. I will meet y'all there so Kevin and I can get the hell out of L.A.."

She walked over to Mike. "Look Mike, I'm sorry that I confronted you like that but I just didn't know what to think. But now that I know my boo is ok, you and Frank can do whatever you want to, but I'm not about to stay around to find out what it's about. Kevin and I are done with this life. We came clean about everything so now it's time for a fresh start."

Mike smiled. It was a nervous smile but he was okay now. "I'm just glad that my boy Kev is good and that you didn't put a cap in my ass. Just gone 'head and get outta here before Frank come. No telling what that nigga up to."

Katrina picked up her purse and put the gun back inside it. She opened the front door and was immediately met with a hard punch to the face. "Sit down bitch, you ain't going nowhere," a voice said.

Mike had already gone back to the kitchen area but ran back up to the front when he heard the commotion. He saw Katrina on the ground and Frank standing over her.

"Frank? Why you hit her, cuz?"

Frank grinned. He saw the blood on her mouth. He stayed silent and all of a sudden thought of something to say. "This bitch killed Kevin."

Both Katrina and Mike were confused. Katrina tried to sit up. "You's a damn lie. I just talked to Jessica. She going to pick him up at his studio now."

Mike chimed in. "Come on, Frank, she's telling the truth. I heard them on the phone."

Frank looked around. "So, why is this gold chain sitting out here? I know that it belongs to Slim, and where the hell did all this blood come from?"

Mike didn't understand. Why was Frank so concerned about Kevin and where did he get his information about Kevin being killed? Mike didn't trust him and if anything did happen to Kevin in the last few minutes, Katrina surely didn't have anything to do with it. He tried to get him to calm down. "Listen man, I heard everything. Slim did come here earlier but Kev was able to escape. We good now."

"Get out," he said to Mike. "Meet me at the crib. I'll be right behind you."

Before he left, he tried to help Katrina up. He then looked at Frank again. "You gonna let her go, right?"

Frank got in his face. "Nigga, I told you to go. Let me take care of this."

Mike decided to leave. Frank taught him everything he knew. It was no point in doubting him now. He figured that Frank had a real reason to want to be there alone with her. On his way out, he noticed a fresh cut on Frank's hand. "Yo, you good?"

"Mike, get the fuck outta here," Frank ordered.

Mike walked out and Frank shut the door. Katrina was still on the ground and showed no sign of being scared. She looked him in his eyes. "What did you do to him?"

Frank ignored her question. "Trina, this ain't even about Kevin. I think you know why I'm here."

"Just tell me, what happened to him?" she begged. "Did you go to his studio?"

Frank put the gun to her face. "Kevin messed up by not taking you out. Who knows who got to him, just know he's dead... Coulda been me, coulda been Antonio, but none of that matters since you won't live to know the truth anyway."

She stood firm. "I ain't scared. Kill me you fat fuck."

Frank had that signature grin across his face. "It's blood for blood."

Katrina knew this wasn't about Kevin. She heard that quote, "blood for blood" before by someone a long time ago. She looked Frank in his eyes. She knew he was ready to kill. She closed her eyes and welcomed death. Her last thought was about Kevin. She was glad to have at least spent her last few months happy. She accepted the fact that she wouldn't walk out alive.

Frank pressed the gun to her skull and let out a single shot. A huge hole split through her head and she was dead immediately.

Frank quickly ran out of the house. He took the stairs all the way down to the lobby and slipped out the back door. His silver Lexus was parked in the back of the building.

CHAPTER TWENTY-FOUR

The Aftermath

Jessica was stuck in traffic and it took her over an hour to reach Kevin's studio. She didn't see him when she arrived. She dialed the number where he last called her from but it was busy. She continued to drive around and didn't see or hear anything. She called Katrina's phone, but she didn't pick up either.

She didn't want to leave the area without hearing from Kevin, so she parked in front of the studio and waited. About ten minutes later, she got out of her car and walked around the building. She started on the left side and she was just about to go on the side where Henry's body was when her phone rang. It was a 562 number. She turned back around and answered. She never saw Henry's body.

The person who called her was a detective and told her he was calling because they saw her number pop up on Katrina's phone.

"Ma'am can you come to the station, please?" he asked.

This caught Jessica by surprise. "What happened to her, is she ok?"

The officer didn't want to let her know what happened over the phone, but after she continued to plead, he ended up telling her that it was a homicide.

Jessica froze in a blank stare with her mouth open. "Are you serious?" she cried out. "When did this happen?"

"We're not sure ma'am. Your number was the last to call her. If you can come by the station, ask for me, Detective Caldwell."

Kevin was nowhere to be found. Even though it was unlikely, she hoped that Kevin didn't have anything to do with her death. She searched for him a little longer before getting in her car and heading to the station.

She went past the studio and through an empty parking lot. She drove past an object. The harder she looked, the more it looked like a person lying in the road. When she looked through her rearview mirror, she confirmed that it was a person. She slammed on the brakes and put the car in reverse. When she got close enough, she got out.

"Kevin!" she cried out once she knew it was him.

His eyes were closed, and he wasn't moving. She started shaking him but nothing worked. Finally, she called the 9-1-1. She panicked as the dispatcher tried to calm her down. "Can you check for a pulse?" the dispatcher asked.

She grabbed his wrist and searched for a pulse. She had never done it before, so she really didn't know what she was doing. The dispatcher tried to explain to her how to do it but she still was unable to find it. She was just about to convince herself that he was gone. Suddenly, she saw a movement from his legs.

"He's alive!" she shouted to the dispatcher.

THE END

Kevin's Chronicles Part 2 is

available now!

Visit www.ronleath.com

Facebook: Author: Ron Leath

Instagram: ronleath

Email: info@ronleath.com

About the Author

Ron Leath was born in Jacksonville, FL and currently lives in Dallas, TX. An unashamed believer in God, a family man and a hard worker, Ron looks to inspire others with his writing. He has been married since 2008 and he and his wife are raising two beautiful children. His mission is to entertain readers with his creative fiction and also show the world that if you believe in yourself, you can accomplish anything.

Be sure to visit www.ronleath.com for updates and new releases!